# TRAIL DUST

Blair Calhoun was hired to drive a trail herd of two thousand longhorns from South Texas into Wyoming Territory – a distance of twelve hundred miles. But with over two hundred miles to go, the herd was stolen by a band of outlaws led by the notorious Mulvaney. The whole of the trail crew, with the exception of Blair and one hand, were murdered. Determined to recover the herd and seek revenge, Blair set out after the cattle thieves. How could one man overcome Mulvaney – and live to tell the tale?

# TRAIL DUST

*by*

## Alan Irwin

**Dales Large Print Books**
Long Preston, North Yorkshire,
BD23 4ND. England.

British Library Cataloguing in Publication Data.

Irwin, Alan
    Trail dust.

    A catalogue record of this book is
    available from the British Library

    ISBN   1-84137-006-1 pbk

First published in Great Britain by Robert Hale Ltd., 1999

Copyright © 1999 by Alan Irwin

Cover illustration © Longaron by arrangement with Norma Editorial S.A.

The right of Alan Irwin to be identified as the author of this work has been asserted by him in accordance with the Copyright Designs and Patents Act, 1998

Published in Large Print 2000 by arrangement with Robert Hale Ltd.

Dales Large Print is an imprint of Library Magna Books Ltd.

Printed and bound in Great Britain by
T.J. (International) Ltd., Cornwall, PL28 8R

# ONE

On the Parminter Ranch, south of San Antonio in Texas, the spring roundup was almost completed. Drover Tex Gardner watched as his hands brought the last of the cows to the place where the herd was to be held overnight in readiness for the start of the trail drive the following morning. Gardner was in his fifties, a stocky bearded man, with a good reputation as a drover.

There were 2,000 longhorns in the herd – a mixture of cows and calves – with a number of steers included to exercise their natural function as leaders on the drive. The herd was destined, not for Eastern food markets via a Kansas railhead, but for Wyoming, 1,200 miles distant, where it would be used as brood stock.

Gardner normally rode with his herd,

5

acting as trail boss, but other commitments had got in the way on this occasion. He had hired eight trail hands as well as a cook and a trail boss, Bob Gregory, who had worked for him in the past.

The drover frowned as he read once more the telegraph message which a ranch hand had brought out to him ten minutes earlier. It told him that Gregory, whom he had expected to arrive that evening, had been thrown from his horse, and had damaged his hip so badly that he wouldn't be able to take charge of the drive.

Gardner rode over towards the chuck wagon which was to accompany the trail drive. Several of the trail hands were chatting with the cook, Henry Green, a short man, bald, bewhiskered, and wearing an apron. Gardner called out to the group as he came to a stop a short distance away from them.

'A word with you, Calhoun,' he shouted.

Blair Calhoun turned and walked up to the drover. He was a man in his late twenties, over average height, and strongly built. There was a capable and cheerful look about him. He wore a knife on his belt and a Colt .45 Peacemaker in a right-hand holster. An old bullet-graze had left a faint scar on his right temple.

He had received this wound during a three-year spell as a deputy sheriff in south-east Texas, during which he had earned respect as a capable lawman, proficient with six-gun and rifle. But seeing the trail herds setting off north each spring had given him the wanderlust and a few years back he had been taken on by Gardner as a trail hand. Three times now he had helped drive a herd up the Chisholm Trail from Texas to Kansas, and during the last two drives he had worked as foreman under the trail boss.

'I've got a proposition for you, Calhoun,' said the drover. 'You know that I hired Bob Gregory as trail boss on this drive because I couldn't make it myself. I've just heard that he can't come, on account of getting himself a busted hip. You've done a good job as ramrod, and I figure you could take Gregory's place and deliver the herd to Wyoming. The job's yours if you want it. The pay's a hundred dollars a month and you can choose your own ramrod. What do you say?'

It didn't take Blair long to consider the offer. He was confident that he was capable of doing the job.

'I'll take it,' he said. 'And the man I want for ramrod is Jake Berry. I've rode with him a couple of times. He's a good man.' He paused for a moment, then continued. 'Can you get another hand to make up the numbers again?' he asked.

'Sure,' replied Gardner, 'I'll hire one as soon as I can and send him on after you. You got all the cows rounded up yet?'

'Yes,' replied Blair.

'Better put the road brand on them now, then,' said the drover. He watched as the men drove the cattle on through a chute, and branded them with the letters 'TP' to mark them as units of a legitimate trail herd, thus distinguishing them from a mixed herd of what might be rustled strays.

They set off the following morning, a day in early April, leaving behind Gardner, who had some business to attend to in Corpus Christi. During the early morning, Blair allowed the cattle to graze for a while as they drifted north. Then the hands gradually manoeuvred the herd into a line of cows four or five abreast, with the steers they had brought along in the lead. The line, heading north, stretched a mile and a half behind the steers.

Blair rode at the head of the line, occasionally riding ahead to scout for pasture and water. The cook drove the chuck wagon just ahead, and to one side of, the leading cows. The wrangler riding level with the rear of the herd, escorted the remuda of sixty-five horses for use by the hands.

Blair had ridden before with the cook, Henry Green, and four of the hands, Wilson, Grant, Messiter and Clark. The other two hands, Dexter and Norton, who had been hired recently in Victoria by Gardner, were strangers to Blair. So far, he had no complaints about the way they were doing their job.

The drag riders behind the line of moving cattle had the worst job, breathing in the dust raised by the herd, and constantly urging slow-moving cows to keep up with the rest. They, together with the riders stationed at intervals alongside the line of moving cows, all combined to keep the herd moving at the right pace and in the right direction. Generally, the pace of the drive would take them ten to twelve miles northward each day.

The cattle were being driven along the Chisholm Cattle Trail, named after a Scottish-Cherokee trader, Jesse Chisholm. Chisholm who had a trading post on the Canadian River in Indian Territory, opened up a wagon road between his trading post and south Kansas. This road eventually formed part of the Chisholm Cattle Trail over which some millions of cows were driven from Texas to the Kansas railheads, and to Wyoming and Canada, during the twenty-year period between the mid-1860s and the mid-1880s.

In the mid-afternoon of the first day of the drive, when the herd approached the place that Blair had chosen for the night's bed ground, he signalled to the hands, who spread apart and allowed the cows to come to a halt. At the same time the cook was starting up a fire for cooking supper.

As darkness was falling, the two hands detailed for the first night watch circled the herd together until the cows bedded down, then continued to circle it in opposite directions until relieved by the second watch. The night horses were specially selected for good night vision and a calm temperament, as well as for their cattle-handling abilities.

## TWO

The following morning the cattle continued on the first leg of the drive that would take them on a 400-mile journey through Texas to the east-flowing Red River, which formed the boundary between Texas and Indian Territory, settled by the Five Civilized Tribes, and also harbouring Kiowa and Comanche warrior tribes. They would pass through Fort Worth on the way.

The day's drive ended without incident. By the time supper had been eaten it was well after dark. Blair, sitting a little way back from the camp-fire, was discussing the following day's journey with Jake Berry. The other hands not on night watch were grouped near the fire, smoking and yarning. An occasional burst of laughter came from the group. From the direction of the bedded herd floated the faint sound of a lullaby coming from one of the night guards circling the cattle.

Suddenly, out of the corner of his eye, Blair saw a small figure stumbling out of the darkness towards the fire. He turned his head and rose quickly to his feet. His companion did the same. As the figure came closer to the fire, stopped, and looked around, they could see that it was that of a young boy, ten or eleven years old. The group of hands by the fire, becoming aware of the boy's presence, turned to stare at him.

Blair walked up to the youth. He could see that he was extremely agitated and on the verge of exhaustion. He wondered where the boy could have come from. They had passed no homesteads or ranch buildings recently.

'Hello, son,' he said. 'Where did you come from? You in trouble?'

The hands walked up as the boy replied. Stumbling over his words, and frequently prompted by Blair, he explained how he came to be there. He told them that his name was Billy Selby and that his father had a small ranch about ten miles east. His father was a horse breeder, he said, and he had a small horse-herd on the ranch.

He told them that earlier in the day he and his sister Beth, who was six years old, had been playing in the hay loft in the barn. Peeping through a small opening in the wall, they had seen three rough looking men ride up to their father and his hand, a man called Binney, as they stood outside the door of the barn. As the riders halted, all three pulled their guns on Binney and Billy's father. The three men had then dismounted and one of them had gone inside the house, to emerge a short time later holding Billy's mother by the arm. He led her over to the others.

Billy had heard one of the three men, who seemed to be the leader, tell his father that they had come to drive off his horse-herd the next morning, and he'd better make no trouble or his wife would suffer. Then one of the men tied the hands of Billy's father and Binney behind them and the leader told Billy's mother to prepare a meal for him and his companions. Then all six went into the house.

Wondering what to do, Billy had continued to watch the house. A few minutes later one of the three strangers came out and walked towards the barn door. Quickly, telling Beth to stay quiet, Billy covered them both with a pile of loose hay. Then, holding Beth's hand, and whispering to her not to speak or move, he waited.

He heard the man walk into the barn, pause for a few moments, then start climbing the ladder to the loft. Again there was silence for a short while. Billy figured that the man was standing on the ladder, with his head inside the loft, looking around. Then he heard the man climb back down the ladder and leave the barn.

Billy had waited a while before throwing the hay aside and resuming his watch on the house. Beth sat beside him. Darkness was now falling, and Billy had decided that he must get help for his parents from somewhere as soon as he could. There was no other ranch or homestead nearby, but Billy had heard his father say that around this time of year thousands of cattle would be moving northward along the Chisholm Trail which passed ten miles to the west of the ranch. He had decided to head for the cattle trail with his sister, in the hope that he would meet up with a trail drive crew.

Billy and Beth had left right after dark, heading west. After they had covered five miles or so, Beth had been too exhausted to go any further, and Billy had left her lying in a recess in the side of a large boulder, with strict instructions to stay there until he returned. Billy had continued until he caught sight of the glow from the camp-fire of Blair's outfit and walked into camp.

Blair spoke to the youngster. 'We'll go back to the ranch with you, Billy,' he said, 'and we'll have to find your sister on the way. It ain't safe for a girl of six to be out there alone. But maybe it ain't going to be easy to find her, 'specially in the dark.'

'I know where I left her,' said Billy, 'and I know she wouldn't move.'

'She's east of here, then?' asked Blair.

'Yes,' said Billy, 'exactly east.'

'Tell you what, Billy,' said Blair, 'you just show me where "exactly east" is.'

Billy took a quick glance at the Big Dipper, clearly visible in the northern sky, then swivelled and pointed. Blair could see that he was pointing as near due east as made no matter.

'My pa showed me how to do this,' said Billy. 'He told me all about the Big Dipper and the North Star.'

Blair spoke to the men. He told the cook to give Billy some food, and the wrangler to saddle a horse for the boy. He told Jake Berry that he was taking four men with him to the Selby ranch, leaving Jake and the rest to look after the herd. He ordered the ramrod to drift the cattle slowly north in the morning, and said that he and the men with

17

him would do their best to catch up with the herd before noon.

Blair and the others left ten minutes later. The men were all armed. They headed due east, Blair keeping them on course, with Billy by his side.

'Let me know – when you think we're anywhere near your sister, Billy,' said Blair, when they had ridden a few miles.

Billy nodded. 'I think we'll soon be crossing a creek,' he said. 'When we do, she'll be somewhere near. D'you think we'll be in time to help my mother and father, Mr Calhoun?'

'I'm hoping so, Billy,' said Blair.

Ten minutes later, they came to a creek running across their path, and halted.

'I think this is the creek,' said Billy, 'but where I crossed it there were three cottonwood trees on this side.'

'Let's find those cottonwoods then,' said Blair, and they first rode north along the creek for about a mile without encountering any trees. Then they turned and rode back

18

along the creek. After a mile and a half they came upon three cottonwoods standing near the edge of the water. Billy looked across the creek at the outline of a large boulder against the night sky, about forty yards distant.

'That's it!' he shouted, excitedly.

They found Beth asleep, lying where Billy had left her. Blair mounted, and one of the hands lifted the girl up into his arms. Then they headed for the ranch.

They stopped about 400 yards from the ranch house. A chink of light was showing through one of the shuttered windows. Blair passed the girl to one of the hands, then dismounted and went ahead on foot to see if a guard had been posted outside the house. He returned fifteen minutes later, lifted Beth down, and told the men to dismount.

'There's no guard,' he said. 'We'll move up behind the barn.'

When they had done this Blair spoke to Billy.

'That chink of light we can see, Billy,' he said. 'Is it coming from the living-room?'

'Yes,' replied Billy.

'I'm going to take a look inside,' said Blair. 'Everybody else stay here.'

He tiptoed over to the window and peeped through the crack in the shutters. He could see two men and a woman sitting on the floor, with hands tied. Their backs were against the opposite wall. They were all awake and there was a look of despair on the woman's face. The three, thought Blair, must be Billy's parents and Binney, the ranch hand.

Sitting at a table in the centre of the room was a big man, roughly dressed and bearded. He was seated in a position which allowed him to keep the three prisoners under close observation, and on the table in front of him lay a Colt .45 revolver.

Looking to the left, Blair could see the ends of two mattresses lying on the floor, side by side, and the legs of two men who were lying on them. The mattresses had obviously been placed, end on, against the wall through which Blair was looking.

Near the far corner of the room Blair could see the door leading to the outside. It was held closed by a stout wooden bar which was resting in two supports fastened to the door frame. He studied the door closely for a short while, then tiptoed back to the others. He described the situation inside the living-room and the positions of the three prisoners and the three men who were holding them captive. Then he spoke to the boy.

'Billy,' he said. 'I want a long, heavy piece of wood that we can use to batter the door of the house down. I think that's going to be the best way to help your father and mother. Is there anything like that around here that we can use?'

'Yes,' said Billy, 'in the barn. I'll show you. It's a corner-post for the corral fence. Pa made it from a tree he chopped down. It's all trimmed, ready to put up.'

Blair went into the barn with Billy and

Beth, and examined the heavy post by the light of a match. It was ideal for the purpose. He told Billy and Beth to stay inside the barn and keep quiet until he came for them. Then he called one of his men inside and together they carried the post out to the others.

'The plan is this,' he told them. 'The five of us will use this post as a battering-ram. We'll take a good long run at the door. We have to break it down first go. If we don't, the plan fails, and Billy's parents and the hand will be in danger. I'll take care of the man sitting at the table with the gun in front of him. You four see to the two men who're lying down. And remember, we've got to keep as quiet as we can right up until the end of this post hits the door.'

He moved over to the window again to confirm that the situation inside the living-room had not changed, then he returned to the others.

Carrying the post, two men on one side and three on the other, they took up a position facing the door and twelve yards away from it. A chink of light showing down the edge of the door gave them a target to aim at in the darkness. At a whispered command from Blair they gripped the post tightly and launched themselves forward, accelerating rapidly, until the end of the ram hit the door squarely in the centre with such force that it fell flat on the floor inside the room.

The man at the table reacted swiftly as he saw Blair leading the others into the room. He grabbed the gun, cocked it, and started bringing it round to bear on Blair. But his move was just a fraction too late. Before his gun was lined up on his target the bullet from Blair's Peacemaker smashed into his chest. The gun fell from his hand and he fell sideways off the chair on to the floor.

The man's two companions were both asleep when the door crashed open. The trail hands relieved them of their guns before they were properly awake, then stood guard over them. Blair went over to the man he had gunned down and picked up his gun. Glancing at the bullet-hole in his victim's vest he could see that the bullet had entered the heart. He walked over to release Selby's wife, then the rancher and Binney.

'My son and daughter,' said the woman. 'Have you...'

'They're all right,' Blair cut in, 'they're outside. I'll bring them here in a minute.'

The body of the dead man was taken to the barn. The two men who had accompanied him were also taken there with their hands tied, and two of Blair's men stood guard over them. Then Blair took the boy and the girl to the house, where they were reunited with their parents.

'We've been sick with worry about the children,' said Jane Selby a little later. 'We knew they were playing in the barn when the three men rode up, and we figured they'd seen the men holding their guns on us. But when they didn't come over to the house we just couldn't imagine what they were doing.'

'It seems,' said Blair, 'that young Billy here has a man's head on his shoulders. He figured you needed help, and he found it. It beats me how a youngster like him found his way to us, then took us back to where Beth was waiting.'

'He's a good boy,' said Pete Selby, putting his arm around Billy's shoulders.

'We'll have to leave soon,' said Blair. 'We've got a trail herd to look after. We'll bury the dead man and take the other two with us. We'll hand them over to the law at San Antonio. We figure to pass by there day after tomorrow.'

'We sure do appreciate the way you've helped us out here,' said Billy's mother. 'We had a bad feeling that maybe those three didn't mean to leave anybody alive when they left here.'

An hour later, Blair and his men left the ranch with the prisoners and rejoined the herd in time for breakfast.

# THREE

The next two days passed without incident and when they reached San Antonio they handed their two prisoners over to the law. It turned out they were wanted for stealing cattle and horses in South Texas. While they were at San Antonio the trail hand that Gardner had promised to send caught up with them. His name was Benteen.

Heading for Fort Worth, a little under 300 miles distant, the drive proceeded steadily for the next two weeks. Grazing was good and the weather was fine. The crew were relaxed, and with a good cook in the outfit, they were eating well and were as contented as it was possible to be while enduring the unavoidable hardships of a trail drive.

Then the peace was shattered by a night-time storm. It had been a sultry evening and the nervous herd had taken a while to bed down. The two hands Benteen and Grant, on the first night watch, were circling the herd when, without any previous flashes or rumblings, there came, from directly overhead, a vivid flash of lightning, followed instantly by a deafening crack of thunder.

The bedded cattle were instantly on their feet and running. The only sounds coming from the stampeding herd were a rumbling sound caused by the pounding of their hooves and the noise produced by the clashing of their horns. Benteen and Grant chased after the cows.

Blair, seated near the fire, and thinking of turning in, heard the rumbling noise and felt a faint vibration of the ground beneath him. He knew instantly what had happened and yelled out orders to the hands. They ran for their horses, mounted, and followed Blair as he chased after the herd.

Benteen and Grant, riding fast, had by now reached a position in front of the stampede. Once there, in an operation fraught with danger, they reined back in an effort to slow the cattle down. Blair and the other hands, arriving at the head of the stampede, on the flank, pressed in on the herd in an effort to turn it.

Looking ahead, Blair could see the shadowy figures of Grant and Benteen, still riding in front of the stampede. He and the others concentrated on their efforts to turn the herd. When pressing in on it proved unsuccessful, they started firing off their revolvers close to the cattle, and eventually this began to have the desired effect. Blair glanced ahead again. Where, shortly before, he had seen the shadowy figures of two riders, now he could only see one.

A mile further on the cattle began to circle, then, a little later, to mill. The stampede was over. Blair rode around the herd, checking up on the hands. There was no sign of Grant. He rode up to Benteen.

'Grant's missing,' he said. 'Did you see him go down?'

'No,' replied Benteen. His voice was strained. 'Like me, he was in front of the stampede, trying to slow the cattle down. One minute he was there, the next he wasn't. I reckon he's a goner, Mr Calhoun. His horse must have put a foot in a prairie-dog hole.'

'We'll come back for him in the morning,' said Blair, and ordered the hands to move the cattle back to the bed ground.

Grant's absence and probable fate cast an air of gloom over the crew, which intensified when, shortly after dawn, they found a shapeless bundle on the ground which was barely recognizable as the remains of a human being. They found Grant's horse, apparently uninjured, grazing nearby.

After Grant had been buried, with a few words from Blair, the trail drive was resumed and they were favoured with good weather until they reached Fort Worth, where Blair bought provisions to replenish their depleted stocks.

There were still almost a hundred miles to

travel before they reached the Red River, which, flowing roughly west to east from New Mexico Territory to its junction with the Mississippi River in Louisiana, formed, over part of its length, the border between Texas and Indian Territory. Grazing was good over this stretch, and in fine weather they made satisfactory progress.

They reached the Red River at Red River Station, a fording point on the south bank of the river, early in the afternoon. Blair and Jake Berry rode up to the bank for a close look at the state of the river. It was easy to see that it was in flood. The water was well up the bank, muddy, and running fast, with debris of various kinds floating on the surface. According to a rider passing by, the river had been normal the previous day and had risen to its present level overnight.

'Looks like we're going to be here for a spell,' said Blair. 'We'll have to wait till the river's safe to cross. We'd sure be asking for trouble if we tried to drive the cattle over now. We'll stay here tonight and see what the situation's like tomorrow.'

But next morning, the water was just as high, and Blair got the hands to move the cattle to some good grass a little way south of the river. Shortly before noon a lone rider appeared from the south and rode up to Blair and the cook, who were standing near the chuck wagon. He looked to be in his mid-twenties and there was a cocky air about him.

'Howdy,' he said. 'I'm looking for the trail boss.'

'That's me,' said Blair. 'I'm Blair Calhoun.'

'Jed Farren,' said the rider. 'I'm trail boss for a herd coming up the Chisholm Trail from Corpus Christi. It should be here in a couple of hours' time. You aiming to cross the river today?'

Blair shook his head. 'No,' he said. 'There's too much water coming down. We're stuck here till the level drops enough to make it safe. But don't take my word for it. Go look for yourself.'

Farren rode to the south bank of the river, then along the bank to Red River Station. Then he rode back to Blair.

'Don't seem too bad,' he said. 'You got any objection to my herd crossing the Red before yours?'

'No objection,' replied Blair, 'but I wouldn't advise it.'

'I've made crossings worse than this,' said Farren. 'If it's done proper, there won't be no trouble.'

'You been a trail boss long?' asked Blair, curiously.

'Long enough,' replied Farren, shortly. 'We'll be along in a couple of hours and I'll take the herd over right away. The owner,' he went on, 'wants the cattle to reach Dodge City just as quick as I can get them there. He's scared there might be a slump coming on the Chicago Cattle Market.'

He rode off south to meet his herd. Blair and the cook watched him go.

'I reckon he's a fool,' said Blair, 'guess there ain't anything we can do about it.'

Just over two hours later the herd appeared in view. It was around the same size as Blair's and as it passed by he could see that there were eight trail hands driving the cattle. Blair and his ramrod rode to the river bank to watch the crossing.

In crossing the river Farren attempted to keep the herd in the same formation as they were used to when being driven on land, but when the cattle reached the unusually deep, turbulent water in the centre of the river, they panicked and started to mill. The hands, unable to swim and fearful for their own safety, were relying entirely on the swimming ability of their mounts. They were powerless to do anything to remedy the situation.

Blair watched one trail hand astride his swimming horse on the edge of the milling herd. Suddenly, a cow swimming beside the horse panicked, collided violently with the horse, and as its head swung to one side, one of the long horns swept the rider out of the saddle. The swift current immediately swept him downstream, arms flailing, until eventually he sank out of sight and did not reappear. The horse struck out for the far bank.

Many of the cattle which were milling frantically in midstream drowned and were swept downriver. The remainder, following one of the big lead steers that decided to head for the north bank, survived.

Farren's cook was an old-timer with experience of many river crossings in the past. Following the orders of the trail boss, and against his better judgement, he had driven the chuck wagon into the river, but realized well before he was half-way across that he would never make it. With some difficulty, helped by one of the trail hands, he managed to turn the team round and drove back to the south bank.

When it was all over Blair could see that only about half the herd had survived. He had no sympathy for the trail boss who, in his opinion, should never have attempted the crossing, and who was responsible for the death of one hand and the loss of half of his herd.

When, later, Blair had a word with Farren's cook, he found out that Farren was the son of the owner of the herd. He had persuaded his father that he was capable of driving the cattle safely to Dodge City.

Farren was forced to hold the remainder of his herd near the north bank until such time as the river level dropped enough to allow the cook to drive the chuck wagon safely over. This he was able to do two days later, just after sun-up. When the cook reached the far side, Farren's crew had a hurried breakfast, then got the cows on the move. Observing Farren's herd through a pair of field glasses, Blair shook his head as he noticed the pace at which the cattle were being driven north.

He took his own herd over the river just before noon without encountering any problems. Then his men drove the herd north at a more leisurely pace than Farren had set for his drive, Blair wishing to put some space between him and the herd in front. Also, he knew that keeping an easy, relaxed pace was a good way of putting some extra weight on the cattle and keeping them healthy.

They now faced a trek of well over 200 miles through Indian Territory, with four river crossings, before they drove over the Kansas border. Had the time been several years earlier, they could have expected trouble from Indian night raids, which had often resulted in stampeding herds, the theft of horses and cattle and the looting of camps.

Since then, the situation had improved, and Blair did not expect to encounter hostile Indians. He was fairly sure, though, that they would meet up with parties of non-belligerent Indians asking for beef. If and when this occurred, he would hand over a steer to ensure a trouble-free drive through that particular area.

They soon settled down again to the routine of the trail drive, the cattle starting the day by grazing as they drifted north for a couple of miles or so. Then the hands put them on the trail and they covered four or five miles before they stopped around noon. The hands took their noon meal while the cattle rested or grazed. After the meal the drive continued until around five o'clock, when the selected bed ground for the night was reached.

During the drive, the remuda, in charge of the wrangler, moved alongside the herd, providing fresh mounts for the cowboys when required. Two or three changes a day might be needed.

When they eventually made their last river crossing in Indian Territory and bedded the herd down on the north side of the Cimarron River, they had lost no beeves, except for six steers handed over to Indians, and the cattle were in excellent condition.

The old Chisholm Trail had originally stretched north from the Cimarron River to Abilene, but a few years earlier the government of Kansas had banned Texas trail herds from this section of the trail because of friction between trail crews and settlers, who, understandably, objected to cattle passing over their land.

This meant that Blair had to take his herd along a cut-off heading north-west from the Cimarron to Dodge City. This route avoided confrontation with settlers, but raised the problem of driving the herd over a hundred-mile stretch between the Cimarron and Arkansas Rivers, which provided little or no water for the cattle.

To avoid harm to the cows because of this it was necessary to halve the time a one-hundred-mile drive would normally take, and Blair achieved this by starting the drive at sun-up each day and continuing it until well after sundown, with a brief noonday break. The drovers, especially the drag riders, even with bandannas pulled over their mouths and noses, suffered badly from the choking cloud of trail dust stirred up by the moving herd.

Blair's luck held. There was a slight rainfall

on the way, and temperatures over this barren area along the cut-off were lower than usual. The tired and thirsty cows arrived at the Arkansas River near Dodge City without stampeding when they first smelled water in the distant river, and without loss. Blair decided to rest them near the river for a couple of days, on good grazing ground.

# FOUR

Figuring that the hands had earned the right to sample the dubious pleasures of Dodge City, Blair told four of them, Wilson, Messiter, Benteen and Norton, that they could ride in that evening and he promised the others the same privilege for the following day. After serving the midday meal the cook drove the chuck wagon into town to buy provisions for the next leg of the drive.

Later in the day the four hands rode into town carrying a small advance on their pay due at trail's end in Wyoming. Blair had decided that he himself would ride into Dodge with the ramrod the following day. After supper he rode over to look at the herd, now peacefully bedded down, and had a quiet word with the two men on night guard.

He returned to the camp and prepared a message for the owner of the cattle in Texas, reporting progress so far. This he would send from Dodge by telegraph the following day. Having done this, he decided it was time to turn in, and he started walking towards the chuck wagon for his bedroll. He paused and turned as four riders rode up to him out of the darkness and dismounted. One of them, Wilson, had a blood-stained bandage on his head. He swayed a little as he stood in front of Blair, supported by Messiter.

'Trouble in Dodge?' asked Blair.

Messiter nodded, and while the cook led Wilson away to attend to his head, he told Blair what had happened.

It seemed that Wilson had got into a poker game in the Long Branch Saloon, which was no surprise to Blair. Buck Wilson was known to him as a first-class poker player and Blair was sure that, if Wilson had wanted, he could have made a good living as a straight gambler. He had the right sort of face and temperament for the job. Rarely, at any time, did his face display a hint of emotion of any kind. In fact, he had a perfect poker face. And to make him an even more formidable opponent, he seemed, more often than not, to be able to guess when another player was bluffing.

Wilson, said Messiter, had got into a game with a cattle buyer and two townsmen when a puncher who had been playing with them pulled out. In a couple of hours he had increased the twenty dollars he had taken into the game (ten dollars of his own, the rest contributed by his companions) to just under 400 dollars, at which point he decided to pull out. He was not a greedy man, and it was getting late.

He collected his winnings and left the saloon in search of his friends who, after watching him play for a time, had gone down the street to a dance-hall to watch a short performance by singer Belle Leroux and her Oriental Dancing Girls. But he never reached them there, and when they came out and found that he had left the Long Branch Saloon some time before, they started looking for him.

They found him eventually, lying in a dark alley, not far from the saloon. He had been savagely pistol-whipped and robbed, and it was a while before he came round.

'Did you tell the town marshal what had happened?' asked Blair.

'We tried to find him,' replied Messiter, 'but it turned out that he and his deputy had ridden out yesterday together. Nobody we spoke to knew where they'd gone or when they'd be back. So we slapped a bandage on Buck's head and brought him back here. On the way, he told us that 400 dollars had been taken, and he had a good idea of the identity of one of the two men who robbed him. I figured we'd better get back here and see you, before we did anything to get the money back.'

'You figured right,' said Blair. 'Let's have a talk with Buck.'

They walked over to the chuck wagon

where Wilson was sitting on a chair. The cook had just finished putting a fresh bandage on his head. 'How is he?' asked Blair.

'He's had a nasty crack on the head,' replied Green, 'but his brain seems to be working OK again. I just asked him what a royal flush was and he had the answer right away. I reckon he'll be all right in a day or so.'

'I hear you got an idea who took the money,' said Blair to Wilson.

Wilson nodded. 'There was a man in the saloon,' he said, 'who was keeping an eye on all the games and throwing out any bad losers who looked like they were going to cause trouble. He was a big man, bald, with a long black moustache and a mean look about him.'

'That's Raven,' said Blair. 'I saw him last year. He's the saloon owner's right-hand man. If I recollect right, the owner's name is Bledsoe.'

'Well,' Wilson went on, 'Raven was one of

the two men who pulled me into the alley and robbed me. I saw him standing behind the man who hit me. The light coming from one of the livery stable windows was shining on his face. There ain't no doubt it was him.'

'I met up with an old friend of mine in Dodge soon after we found Buck,' said Messiter. 'We used to punch cows together on the Lazy Y in South Texas. He works in a livery stable in Dodge. He told me that as far as the law around here is concerned, County Sheriff Benson is a good, reliable lawman to turn to in case of any trouble outside the city limits. But he said that he was pretty sure we wouldn't get any help from Black, the town marshal in Dodge, in catching the men who robbed Buck. He reckoned the marshal and his deputy Brand are in the pay of some of the saloon owners, and Bledsoe is one of them. He said he was sure that Black was paid to turn a blind eye on the dirty tricks some saloon owners used to boost their profits.'

Blair, who had been a conscientious

lawman himself, knew that although the majority of peace officers were men of integrity, there were some who were more interested in lining their own pockets than in upholding the law.

'That tallies with what I heard last year,' he said, 'so we're lucky the marshal and his deputy are out of town. It gives us a chance to get that money back ourselves. There ain't no doubt that it's ended up in Bledsoe's hands.

'I remember from when I was in the saloon last year,' he went on, 'that Bledsoe was on the ground floor watching the action most of the time, but now and again he went into a room opposite the top of the stairs to the upper floor. Somebody told me he lives and sleeps in that room and uses it as an office as well. That's where he'll hold his money before he banks it.'

'I saw him go in and out of that room a couple of times while we were there,' said Messiter, 'but it ain't possible to get in there without being seen by somebody.'

'Maybe it is,' said Blair, trying to visualize the external features of the saloon. He went on to explain his plan to the others. 'We can't do it till after dark tomorrow,' he concluded, 'and I only need one man with me.' He turned to Dexter, who was one of the men who had not gone into Dodge earlier. 'You'd better come along,' he said. 'And the other men riding in tomorrow must be back here well before nightfall.'

'When do we start moving the herd?' asked Jake.

'The morning after we get back with the money,' replied Blair.

The two men rode into Dodge just after dark, each carrying a large sack fastened to his horse behind the saddle. Looking in through one of the windows of the Long Branch Saloon which overlooked the street, they could see that the place was fairly crowded, although the street outside was quiet.

They untied the two sacks, then, making sure that they were unobserved, they dumped the contents, a mixture of dried brush, twigs and small branches, out of sight under the boardwalk at the front of the saloon, and pushed it up against the wall planking. They left a can of coal oil near the pile, then went inside the saloon, where they stood at the bar and ordered a couple of beers.

Looking around, Blair could see that both Bledsoe and Raven were on the ground floor. Bledsoe was seated at a table with two other men, and Raven was circulating, keeping an eye on the gambling activities. Blair pointed both men out to Dexter, then looked up the stairs to the door of Bledsoe's room. Looking at the other doors on the landing, he could see that the saloon owner's room was the middle one of five rooms on the east side of the building.

He and Dexter went outside and walked along the front of the saloon and into an alley which ran along the east side of the building. They looked up at the railed-in veranda above, which could be accessed only from five rooms, which had glass doors leading on to it. The centre room was Bledsoe's. The veranda was supported by stout timber pillars.

'I'm going to wait up there,' said Blair. 'You move the horses down the street to that hitching rail outside the store. Then empty the oil can on to that stuff under the boardwalk and light it. But make sure nobody sees you. As soon as Bedsloe realises his place is in danger of burning, let me know. When you've done that, go and wait for me outside the store. While Bledsoe's making sure the fire's put out I'll go into his room.'

They looked up and down the street to make sure no one was approaching the alley, then Blair climbed on to Dexter's shoulders and scrambled up the upper half of one of the pillars, over the veranda rail, and on to the veranda itself. He ran over to the door leading to Bledsoe's room and crouched against it.

A glimmer of light came from a narrow

gap in the drawn curtains on the other side of the door, but the gap was not wide enough to enable him to see if anybody was in the room. He stayed where he was, waiting for Dexter to return.

Before this happened, he heard a sudden burst of shouting from the front of the saloon, and saw the glow from the flames illuminating the street at the end of the alley. Shortly after this, hearing a faint call from Dexter below, he moved over to the rail.

'Bledsoe and Raven are both outside,' said Dexter, then left the alley and headed for the store.

Blair went back to the door of Bledsoe's room, taking from his belt a strong steel chisel with a thin wide blade, which he had taken from the chuck wagon. He inserted the blade in the gap between the door and the frame, and exerting all his strength, he managed to force the door open. He parted the curtains and looked into the room. It was empty.

He walked in and looked around. He was

relieved when a search revealed no sign of a locked safe. He looked at the strongly built desk standing against one wall of the room, and walked over to it. Two of the drawers were locked. The first of these, when forced open with the chisel, revealed a number of documents. The second contained papers and a wad of banknotes.

Blair extracted notes to the value of 600 dollars from the bundle and replaced the remainder in the drawer. He figured that the extra 200 dollars was due to Wilson for the knock on the head. He pushed the drawers to and walked out on to the veranda, closing the curtains and the door behind him.

Unobserved, he climbed down from the veranda and walked out of the alley into the street, where he could see that the fire was being brought under control by buckets of water fetched from somewhere along the street. He could see Bledsoe and Raven standing in the street shouting instructions to the men fighting the flames. He walked along to the store where Dexter was waiting and the two men rode back to the herd, where the money was divided between Wilson and the men who had gone into town with him.

The following morning they set out on the last leg of the drive, which would take them over the Western Trail through Kansas and Nebraska to Wyoming, just under 400 miles distant. They made good progress on the first day and on the morning of the second day. During the noon stop, Blair, who had just finished his dinner, saw a couple of riders coming towards them from the south. He got his gunbelt from the chuck wagon and buckled it on.

The riders drew closer and when Blair saw the badges on the men's vests he recognized the bigger of the two as Black, town marshal of Dodge, whom he had seen in Dodge the previous year. He spoke to the cook, who started to rummage in the chuck wagon. Then he turned to watch the approaching riders.

Black was a big man, red-faced and carrying too much fat. His deputy, a man called Brand, who was barely out of his teens, was wearing a couple of fancy six-guns. Blair walked towards the two lawmen, who stopped in front of him, then dismounted.

'You the trail boss?' asked Black abruptly.

Blair nodded. 'The name's Calhoun,' he said.

'I'm taking you and one of your hands back to Dodge,' said Black. 'The hand I want is the one who was with you in Dodge two days ago. Saddle up, and we'll be on our way.'

'I'm a mite curious as to why you want us to go along with you, Marshal,' said Blair.

'I'm charging you both with robbery and arson,' said Black. 'You were both seen in the Long Branch Saloon around the time that it was set on fire and the saloon owner was robbed.'

'I *was* in town with one of my men, Dexter, two days ago,' said Blair, 'but did anybody actually see us starting a fire and committing a robbery?'

'I'm sure I can find some witnesses,' said Black.

'I'm sure you can,' said Blair, 'but what about a motive? Why should a trail boss and a trail hand have done those things?'

'There's been enough talk,' said Black, his face flushing with anger. 'You and Dexter are coming along with us right now. And that money you stole. Be sure you bring it with you.'

The hands of the marshal and his deputy hovered near the handles of their six-guns. Brand looked almost as though he was wishing for trouble.

Blair spoke slowly and distinctly.

'Black,' he said. 'I happen to know just what kind of a lawman you are. You take money for turning a blind eye on a lot of the criminal activities in Dodge. You look after your own interests but you don't give a damn about the interests of the ordinary citizens you're supposed to be protecting.

And looking at your deputy, I'm pretty sure he's just as rotten a lawman as you are yourself.

'We're not going with you,' he went on. 'For one thing you're a town marshal, and you ain't got no jurisdiction here. You're a long way from the town limits of Dodge. If you want to go and find County Sheriff Benson and tell him your story and ask him to come out here and see me, I'll talk it over with him. I've heard he's an honest man.'

Black's face purpled with anger. He spoke to his companion.

'Deputy,' he said. 'We're arresting this man. You know what to do.'

Brand, who had given every indication of straining at the leash, pulled his right-hand gun, supremely confident in his ability to outdraw the man in front of him. But before he had lined up his six-gun on Blair, the deputy looked down in shocked disbelief as a bullet from Blair's revolver tore through the flesh of his right forearm, above the wrist.

Black's jaw dropped and he started to pull his own gun, but changed his mind when the cook, approaching him from behind, jammed the twin barrels of a 10-gauge shotgun into his side.

'Not a good idea, Black,' said Blair. 'Just stay quiet for a minute.'

He walked over to Brand, who, holding his wounded arm, had abandoned any idea of pulling his second gun. Blair bent down to pick up the deputy's six-gun, removed the ammunition from it, and replaced it in the holster from which Brand had drawn it. He did the same with the deputy's second gun. Then he glanced at the wound on Brand's arm. He could see that it was only superficial.

'You two had better go back where you belong,' he said. 'And like I told you, we'll be happy to talk to the sheriff any time. Tell him we're heading for Ogallala.' As he spoke, Blair knew it was most unlikely that Black would take the matter up with Sheriff Benson.

56

'This ain't the last of this, Calhoun,' said Black, rage boiling up inside him.

'Get moving,' said Blair, and the two men mounted and headed south. Blair watched them until they disappeared from view. Then he walked over to the cook, who was returning the shotgun to the chuck wagon. The hands who had observed the proceedings were standing by the chuck wagon discussing the gun-handling expertise of the trail boss and the chagrin of Black and his deputy.

'You did a good job there, Henry,' said Blair, 'backing me up like that. I thought for a minute I was going to have to fire at the marshal as well.'

'What do we do now?' asked the cook.

'Why, we carry on with the drive, of course,' replied Blair, and ordered the hands to put the herd back on the trail. Then he rode ahead to choose a bed ground for the night.

# FIVE

All went well during the next fifteen days.
Then, on the afternoon of the sixteenth day,
just after they had crossed the border into
Nebraska, they were hit by a thunderstorm
of considerable ferocity. The storm had
been heading their way for some time and
the hands were apprehensive. Death by
lightning strike, of both cattle and men, was
not unknown on the cattle trails.

At the height of the storm, Norton was
riding flank, close to the herd, when a vivid
lightning discharge flashed to the earth
close by, accompanied by a deafening crack
of thunder. Three cows were killed, as well
as Norton's mount. Norton himself was
badly burnt, from a point underneath his
belt buckle to the outside of his left leg, then
down this leg to the top of his left boot. A

stampede was narrowly avoided.

The cook stopped the chuck wagon and ran back to help Norton who was lying on the ground. He examined the burns and didn't like what he saw. He helped Norton on to the chuck wagon seat and drove the wagon the short distance to the next bed ground. Once there, he gave Norton water to drink and cleaned the affected area as well as he could, before applying a wet bandage to ease the pain. Then, seeing that Blair was approaching, he threw a blanket over the injured man and walked over to meet the trail boss.

'It sure don't look good,' he said. 'He's going to have a bad scar for the rest of his life. I've done what I can for now, but I reckon Cal Norton should see a doctor as soon as we're anywhere near one. The trouble is that infection's likely to set in.'

'First thing tomorrow,' said Blair, 'I'll take him to Ashton. That's about thirty miles north-west of here. It's a small town, but I was told there's a doctor there.'

'That's right,' said the cook, 'but until you see the doctor, make sure Cal drinks a little water every now and then.'

'I'll do that,' said Blair, then walked over to the injured man and looked down at him.

'I'm figuring to take you to the doctor in Ashton first thing tomorrow, Cal,' he said. 'You reckon you'll be able to ride a horse?'

'Sure I will,' replied Norton.

'Rest if you can,' said Blair. 'We'll ride at sun-up.'

But later on, when he went to see Norton again, he found the hand was in considerable pain. He called Jake Berry over.

'I'm taking Cal to the doctor now,' he said. 'The sooner he sees one, the better. It ain't likely I'll be back here by morning, so you'd better take the herd on to the next bed ground tomorrow and I'll meet up with you there. It's about ten miles north of here, where a creek crosses the trail. I reckon Cal might have to stay in Ashton for a spell. That burn he's got is a pretty bad one.'

Blair and Norton set off just after

midnight. The cook and the ramrod watched them disappear into the darkness, then they both turned in. The two night guards, Messiter and Clark, were circling the bedded herd in opposite directions, in a basin, south of the camp, which was just about large enough to accommodate the herd. The sides of the basin were covered with brush.

At about one hour after midnight the two guards were on opposite sides of the herd, out of each other's sight, when two men ran out of the brush towards Messiter. As the guard's horse reared in fright, one of the men caught its reins, and the other pulled Messiter out of the saddle and struck him on the head with the barrel of his pistol as the trail hand fell to the ground.

Moments later, Messiter, trussed and gagged, was lying helpless on the ground and his mount was tied to a small tree nearby. Some of the cattle around, which had risen to their feet during the disturbance, looked towards the intruders and their victim.

At the same time that Messiter was attacked, exactly the same thing was happening to Clark, on the other side of the herd.

When both the night guards had been put out of action, all four attackers climbed out of the basin and joined up with the two mounted men who were waiting there, holding their horses. They mounted, and all six riders moved quietly towards the camp, one slightly in the lead.

Jake Berry, the cook, and the other three trail hands, tired after a hard day, were all sound asleep. The cook was lying close to the chuck wagon. The others were scattered between the wagon and the fire. All were dimly visible in the light from the fire.

The six riders paused at a signal from their leader, who looked across the fire at the sleeping men beyond it. Then they all dismounted, and while one of them held the horses, the other five moved stealthily forward, each of them targeting one of the men lying asleep on the ground. Suddenly, as the cook stirred and coughed, the five men froze, until he turned over and resumed his slumber. Then they advanced again and over the last eight yards they made a concerted rush which brought each one up to his intended victim at the same time. Deliberately, they shot each one of the five sleeping men through the head.

The leader spoke to two of his men, who went for their horses and rode off towards the south. A short time after they left, two pistol shots were heard by the others, the sounds coming from the direction of the basin in which the cattle were being held.

Blair and Norton arrived in Ashton just after four in the morning. Seeing a small hotel on the one and only street, with a light on inside, they stopped outside it and Blair dismounted and hammered on the door. It was opened after a short delay by the owner Carl Benz, yawning and dressed in his night attire.

'I've got a man here,' said Blair, 'who needs to see a doctor. I heard that you've got one in this town. Where can I find him?'

Benz peered at Norton, still sitting on his horse, head bowed.

'Doc Merton's place is on the right, further along the street,' he said. 'You'll see his shingle outside. But he ain't there now. He's been called to a ranch a fair way west of here where two men were badly shot. He left about midnight. He told me it'd be noon today, maybe later, before he showed up again. What's the matter with your friend?'

'Hit by lightning,' replied Blair. 'Burnt pretty bad. You got a room we can have?'

'Sure,' replied Benz. 'Number four. There's two beds in there. You help your friend up there while I take your horses over to the livery stable. There'll be some breakfast on the go at seven o'clock.'

'Thanks,' said Blair. He helped Norton down from his horse and up the stairs to the room, where the trail hand collapsed on to one of the beds. Blair looked down at him.

Norton didn't look too good, he thought. He wondered if he should change the bandages, but decided that maybe it had better wait until the doctor took a look at the damage.

Both men lay awake until breakfast time. Blair took food up to Norton, but the trail hand had little appetite for it. Blair stayed with him until the doctor finally drove his buggy into town just after two in the afternoon. Benz saw him arrive and told Blair, who walked up to the buggy as it stopped outside the doctor's house. As Merton stepped down, Blair introduced himself, and told the doctor about Norton.

'I'm a mite tired,' said Merton, a tall, thin man, dressed in black. 'I've just had a long drive to see to a couple of ranch hands who fell out and decided to ventilate one another. I had to dig lead out of both of them.

'But I reckon,' he went on, 'that I'd better see that trail hand of yours right away. Burns can be nasty. I'll see you at the hotel in ten minutes.'

When the doctor arrived at the hotel he took the bandages off and closely examined the area of charred skin extending from waist to ankle, down one leg. Then he took Blair aside.

'One thing's certain,' he said. 'This is a bad burn. This man won't be fit for riding for a while. Infection is what we've got to worry about. You being a trail boss I guess you've got to get back to your herd, so if you like he can stay in my place till he's fit to ride. We'll take him there now, then I'll tend to the wound and cover it up properly again.'

'I sure appreciate your offer, Doc,' said Blair. 'I'll leave money with Norton for his keep and treatment, and I'll leave his horse in the livery stable. He can catch up with us when he's fit again.'

As soon as they had transferred Norton to a bed in a small room at the doctor's house, Blair took his leave of them both and headed for the place where he had told the ramrod to bed the cattle down for the night. He arrived there around five o'clock, to find no sign of the herd, which should have been close by that time.

He started riding towards the place where he had last seen the herd, but he had seen no sign of it by the time he reached the previous night's bed ground. He approached the camp slowly. He could see no camp-fire. The sun had gone down two hours earlier, but as he approached the place where the fire had been located, there was enough light to show him that there was no chuck wagon nearby.

He rode on a little further, then stopped abruptly. On the ground in front of him was a shapeless object which could have been the blanket-covered body of a sleeping man. He called out, but the object remained motionless. He dismounted, bent down, grasped the shoulder showing outside the blanket, and shook it.

Immediately, from the stiffness of the body, he knew that the man was dead, and had been for some time. He struck a match and found himself looking into the face of his ramrod. A bullet-hole in the centre of his forehead showed how Jake had died. Then, one by one, Blair found the bodies of the cook, Wilson, Benteen and Dexter. They had all died the same way, shot through the head while lying down, probably asleep.

That left Messiter and Clark, thought Blair, sickened by what he had just found. They had been on night guard. Quickly he mounted his horse and rode to the basin where the herd had been held the previous night. The herd was gone, but he found the bodies of the two trail hands, still trussed and gagged, and each with a bullet wound in the head.

Badly shaken by the butchery that had taken place, Blair stood by his horse for a while. It was clear to him that the men who had committed this act of savagery must be brought to book.

## SIX

Before setting out on the trail of the rustlers, Blair knew that he must get some food supplies and ammunition. He rode back to Ashton, arriving around midnight, and took a room at the hotel, explaining to Benz why he was back. Benz told him that the nearest lawman was a county sheriff, too far away to be of any immediate help.

In the morning, Blair went to the store and got the items he needed. Then he went along to the doctor's house. Merton was surprised to see him. When Blair told him of the reason for his return, he shook his head in disbelief.

'I ain't heard of anything like that around here before,' he said. 'D'you reckon they were Indians?'

'No,' replied Blair. 'What happened out

there wasn't the Indian way of killing. They were white men for sure. I'm going to get on their trail right away. But first, I'll have a word with Norton. How's he doing?'

'The pain ain't so bad this morning,' said Merton, 'but it's too early to say whether infection's going to be a problem.'

Blair broke the news to Norton about the murder of his comrades and told him that he was going to follow the tracks of the herd. When Norton recovered a little from the shock he asked Blair what he should do when he was fit to ride.

'Ride out to where we left the cattle,' said Blair, 'then follow the tracks of the herd from there. Somewhere along those tracks there's a chance that you'll find me. But watch out for the rustlers.'

Blair left shortly after, heading for the place where the trail hands had been murdered. When he arrived there he moved the bodies of Messiter and Clark from the basin to the place where the other five bodies were lying. Taking a spade which he had bought in Ashton, he dug a large grave and laid the seven bodies in it. After resting a short while he filled the hole in.

When he had finished he stood for a short while looking down at the grave of men he had come to respect and trust, some of them friends of long standing, whose lives had been terminated so savagely and abruptly. He was resolved to do his best to recover the herd for its owner and to make the murderers pay for their crime.

Riding around the rim of the basin, Blair soon found the tracks left by the stolen herd as they were driven off. They diverged from the trail which the herd had been following, and struck off in a north-easterly direction. Blair followed them until he came to the place where the herd had bedded down for the night. He examined the area closely.

He could not be sure, but he guessed that there were six or seven men with the herd. He continued to follow the tracks of the stolen cattle, still heading north-east. When darkness fell he guessed that the bed ground was not more than a few miles in front of him. He rode more cautiously now, and paused when he saw the feeble glow of a camp-fire far ahead.

He wondered whether the men ahead of him were expecting pursuit. He figured they must have been shadowing the herd for a while before stealing it, but not too closely, otherwise they would have been spotted. It was pretty dark when he and Norton had left for Ashton and they had seen no sign of the rustlers. Probably, thought Blair, they had ridden into camp well after he and Norton had left, and were under the impression that they had killed the trail boss and all the crew. All the same, he decided to approach the camp with great caution.

He swung off the trail, completed a large half-circle till he met up with the trail again on the other side of the rustlers' camp, then cautiously approached the camp-fire from the north-east. First, he came to the bedded herd which was located on a flat, grassy area ringed with trees. From the shelter of these

Blair watched the dim shapes of the two night guards as they passed by him, slowly circling the herd in opposite directions. The sky was clear and the moon was shining.

Leaving the herd behind him, Blair rode on a short distance till he came to within fifty yards of the camp-fire. He dismounted and tied his horse to a tree. He advanced on foot, and crouched behind a small patch of brush. From this position he could see into the small clearing surrounding the fire. There were three blanket-covered figures lying on the ground, and just beyond them he could see the chuck wagon which had accompanied the herd from Texas, recognizable by the large white patch on the canvas cover.

Blair returned to his horse, then rode back to the herd, keeping out of sight of the two guards. He dismounted and secured his horse. Then, hiding in the trees near the edge of the herd, he watched as the guards each made one circuit of the herd. Then, after one of the guards had passed close by him, he waited for the other to appear. He estimated that this would be when the guard who had just passed was on the far side of the herd.

He stayed in hiding until the rider had walked his horse past him. Then he stepped out, holding his lariat, with the loop in his right hand. He sent the loop flying towards the rustler from behind, to settle over the guard's head and shoulders. He pulled hard on the rope, pinning the man's arms to his sides, and yanked him out of the saddle. But as the man hit the ground, the loop slackened a little and he grasped the handle of his gun and turned to face Blair. Blair dropped the lariat, drew his knife, and before the rustler could fire his revolver the long blade of the knife, thrown with unerring accuracy by Blair, had penetrated his heart.

Hurriedly, Blair changed his own hat for the rustler's, then pulled the body into the trees. He mounted the man's horse, which had a distinctive white blaze running down its face, and continued walking it around the herd in the same direction as that which had been followed by his victim.

It was not long before he saw the other guard approaching him through the darkness. He bent his head down a little, to hide his face, and rode slowly towards the rustler, intending to pistol-whip him if he could get close enough. But just before they met, something about the man in front of him alerted the guard and he went for his six-gun. Once again Blair threw his knife and put the rustler out of action before he was able to fire his gun and alert the men around the camp-fire.

The man fell from his horse. Blair dismounted and bent over him. He died as Blair watched. Blair retrieved his knife, dragged the man's body into the trees out of sight, and secured the guards' horses close by. He found the guns belonging to the two men and threw them into the middle of a dense patch of brush. Then he mounted his own horse and rode back towards the camp-fire and the remaining rustlers.

He returned to the same position from which he had observed them earlier. They were fairly widely spaced on the ground and all appeared to be sleeping soundly. He had no doubt that all were armed and ready to start shooting at the first sign of danger. He was sure that two of them would be scheduled, at some time, to relieve the two men guarding the cattle. He decided to wait until these two men left the clearing, so allowing him to deal first with the rustler left sleeping by the fire, then with the other two men when they discovered that there were no men guarding the herd.

Half an hour passed as Blair squatted behind the patch of brush, his eyes on the blanketed figures of the three sleeping men. Then, at the slightest of sounds behind him, he started to twist round and his hand reached for his Peacemaker. But it was too late. He was knocked violently forward, to lie face-down on the ground, and a heavy weight pinned him down. At the same time the muzzle of a six-gun was jammed into the side of his neck.

'Move, and you're dead,' growled the man lying on top of him.

Blair lay still, as the man took his Peacemaker and knife, then stood up. He ordered Blair to stand up and face the fire, while he kept the barrel of his gun jammed against the back of the trail boss. He called out to the three sleeping men. They stirred, reached for their guns, and sat up, looking towards him.

'Look what we've got here,' he said, prodding Blair in the back with his gun, and ordering him to walk towards the fire. The three men rose and walked towards Blair and the man behind him. They all came to a halt.

The man who had just captured Blair was a half-breed called Lasko. He was a tall, bearded, heavy man, surprisingly light on his feet. The three men standing in front of Blair were, with Lasko, members of an infamous gang of rustlers, all wanted by the law, who, as Blair knew, thought nothing of murder if that was necessary to achieve their ends.

One of the three was the leader of the gang, Mulvaney. A slightly built man, it was his eyes which first caught the attention. They were a very pale, unnatural blue. Then, a close look at his face gave the strong impression that this was an evil, ruthless man. The two men by his side were called Barnet and Slater, both tough-looking characters with several days' growth of stubble on their faces.

'I've got bad news,' said Lasko to Mulvaney. 'There ain't no guard on the cattle. I got back from Drayton about half an hour ago with them supplies you wanted. When I passed the herd, there weren't no sign of Glade or Henty, so I scouted round for a while. I found them both lying in the trees. They'd been knifed. They're both dead.' He held up the knife he'd just taken from Blair. 'And I reckon this is what did it. I just found it on this man. I figured the killer might be somewhere around the camp, and sure enough I found him over there, watching you three. Guess he never figured on me riding in like I did.'

Mulvaney's face contorted with rage as he regarded Blair, and there was a look in his cold eyes which boded ill for the prisoner. 'Do we know who this man is?' he asked Lasko, harshly. 'His horse,' replied Lasko, 'has the same brand on it as the horses in the remuda we brought along with the herd.'

'So it looks like we didn't get them all,' said Mulvaney, 'and this man chases after us on his own, aiming to get the herd back.'

'He must be crazy,' said Lasko, 'bucking all six of the Mulvaney gang.'

'Maybe so,' said Mulvaney, 'but there's only four now. You sure nobody came with him?'

'I'm sure,' replied Lasko. 'Should I finish him off now?'

Mulvaney thought for a moment. Then he shook his head. 'No,' he said, 'we're even more short-handed now we've lost two men. We could do with his help on the drive. He can drive the chuck wagon. We'll tie him on to the seat so he can't leave the wagon, and the point rider can keep an eye on him. If he don't do what he's told, we'll kill him.

'Search him,' Mulvaney went on, 'and see if he's got any papers on him.'

Lasko did this, and handed over to the gang leader some papers he found in Blair's vest pocket. Mulvaney read them with interest, then spoke to Blair.

'According to these papers,' he said, 'you're the trail boss of the outfit we took the herd from. Blair Calhoun by name. Can't think where you were at the time. But let me make one thing plain. Do as you're told tomorrow, or you're dead.'

Five minutes later, Blair, tied hand and foot and firmly lashed to the chuck wagon wheel, watched as Barnet and Slater left to mount guard over the herd for the remainder of the night. Blair looked over at Mulvaney, as the man who had ordered the murder of his trail hands lay down, pulled a blanket over himself, and appeared to fall into instant slumber.

Blair figured that he had better play along with Mulvaney's idea that he should drive the chuck wagon. If he stayed alive long enough, maybe a chance to turn the tables would come along. He dozed, uncomfortably, until Lasko, who was acting as cook, got up and started seeing to the breakfast. A little later, Mulvaney rose and walked over to Blair. He stood looking down at the prisoner.

'Remember what I told you earlier,' he said. Then he moved away.

After he had been given breakfast, and before the rustlers got the herd moving, Blair was escorted to the bed ground and ordered to dig a grave for Henty and Glade. When he had filled this in he was taken back to the chuck wagon and tied on the seat. The rustlers put the herd back on the trail and Blair drove the chuck wagon close to, and slightly ahead of, the point rider.

The herd was pretty well-behaved by now, after weeks on the trail, and they made good progress that day and on the following two. The outlaws kept a close watch on Blair and there had been no opportunity for him to escape. On the third day, at supper, Blair overheard Mulvaney and Lasko talking. From what he heard, it seemed that the rustlers were going to hand the herd over to a man called Hiram Trent at some time in the near future, exactly when was not clear. When the handover took place, thought Blair, Mulvaney would have no further need of him, and he would almost certainly share the fate of his murdered trail hands. The time left for him to make his escape was obviously limited.

As was usual, Blair ate his supper sitting against the chuck wagon wheel, with feet tied and hands free. The wheel behind him was resting close to a small patch of very light sandy soil, and during supper Blair surreptitiously formed a small pile of sand by his side and laid his right hand on top of it when he had finished eating.

Mulvaney and Lasko ate a hurried meal, then left to watch over the herd. When Barnet and Slater had finished their own meal, they put more wood on the fire, then walked up to Blair to tie his hands and lash him to the wagon wheel for the night. Barnet was carrying a length of rope and he started to uncoil it as he came up to Blair. Slater was just behind him.

'This chuck wagon wheel I'm sitting against,' said Blair. 'It ain't going to last more'n a few hours on the trail. I've just noticed there's a bad split in the rim and three of the spokes are loose. See for yourselves.' He pointed down to his right.

Barnet cursed, and he and Slater bent forward together to have a close look at the wheel in the dim light. Blair took a handful of sand in his right hand and flung it into the faces of the two rustlers, at the same time grabbing with his left hand for the gun in Barnet's holster. He pulled it free just before Barnet, partially blinded, jerked backwards.

Blair transferred the gun to his right hand and shot Slater as the rustler, blinded in one eye, was drawing his gun. Slater fell on the ground, dropping his revolver as he did so. It landed close to his partner's feet. Desperately Barnet bent down and grabbed it, but before he could take aim at the prisoner, Blair shot him in the chest.

Blair knew that it would only be a short while before Mulvaney and Lasko would be arriving to investigate the shooting. He glanced at the two rustlers lying on the ground. Both were motionless. Quickly, he undid the rope around his ankles, picked Slater's gun off the ground, and ran to the far side of the chuck wagon, arriving just before Mulvaney and Lasko, guns in hand, rode into the clearing.

The two rustlers rode up to the two bodies lying on the ground.

'Have a look at them, Lasko,' ordered Mulvaney, and kept watch while the half-breed dismounted, sheathed his gun, and bent over the two men on the ground, in turn.

'They're both dead,' said Lasko. 'It's Calhoun's doing. Can't think how he managed to get the better of those two.'

'We've got to find him,' said Mulvaney, his voice thick with rage. 'He can't have gone far.'

'I'm right here, Mulvaney,' shouted Blair, running out from behind the chuck wagon, gun in hand, to face the two rustlers.

Mulvaney, already holding a gun, started bringing it up to bear on Blair. But his horse, startled by Blair's sudden appearance, shied away, and before the rustler was able to fire in the direction of the trail boss, Blair's bullet nicked Mulvaney's arm and lodged in his right side. He dropped his gun and slumped forward on to the horse's neck as the animal took fright and ran off.

Blair had no time to take a second shot at Mulvaney before turning his attention to Lasko. When Blair had shouted, the half-breed's back was towards him. Lasko turned round, drawing his gun as he did so, but his hurried shot missed Blair, whose second shot drilled into the rustler's chest before he could fire again.

Lasko fell, shot through the heart. Blair picked up the rustler's six-gun, then looked in the direction in which Mulvaney's horse had taken off. He wondered whether the outlaw was still alive, and if so, whether he had managed to stay on his horse. He knew that the gang leader was weaponless. He had dropped his six-gun when he was shot and Blair had noticed that there was no rifle in his saddle holster. So even if he was close by, and alive, he should present no danger, provided that Blair was vigilant.

Blair went for his horse and rode over to the herd, keeping an eye open for Mulvaney. The cattle were quiet and all bedded down. He stayed near the herd for the rest of the night, wondering how a one-man outfit could possibly get a herd of 2,000 head to its destination.

## SEVEN

When daylight came Blair had a look round for any signs of Mulvaney. He found horse tracks leading north-east, which he was sure had been left by the gang leader's mount, and here and there, close to the tracks, were signs of blood. He followed the tracks for half a mile, at which point they turned and headed east. He followed them for a further mile in that direction, then turned and rode back to the herd. He was reasonably sure that Mulvaney had been wounded and had left the area.

Although Blair had every intention of seeing that the man who had brutally ordered the murders of his hands was eventually brought to book, he knew that his first task was to deliver the herd. When he got back to it, he found the cattle grazing contentedly near the bed ground. He spent some time burying the bodies of the three dead outlaws, then prepared a meal. He had just finished eating this when he saw a distant rider approaching from the south-west.

He checked his Peacemaker and rifle, both of which he had found stowed away in the chuck wagon, and awaited the rider's arrival. There was something familiar about him, and it was not long before he realized that the man approaching him was Norton, the hand who had been injured by lightning. He waved his arm in greeting.

Norton rode up to Blair and dismounted. He looked around. 'You alone?' he asked.

'I sure am,' replied Blair. 'I was just sitting here wondering how one man can get this herd to Wyoming. Now I'm wondering how two men can do the same thing. It just ain't possible.' He went on to tell Norton of his experiences since he had left Ashton with the intention of following the herd. Then he asked Norton about his injured leg.

'It's badly scarred for life,' said Norton, 'and it still hurts some. But I can still use it. Doc Merton said I was lucky. It could have turned out worse. He figured I was fit to ride, so I just followed the tracks of the herd till I got here.

'Looks like you had a good slice of luck yourself,' he went on, 'getting the better of those rustlers like you did.'

'You're right,' said Blair, 'for a while ' He broke off as he spotted a distant group of riders heading in their direction. He drew Norton's attention to them.

'Let's hope we're not in for any more trouble,' he said. 'Check your gun, let me do the talking, and follow any play I make.'

As the group drew closer they could see that there were five riders, and even at a distance, Blair had a strong impression that they were cowboys. He knew this was so when they drew even closer and he recognized one of them as a Texan, Herb Myers, who had been a trail hand on the first trail drive that Blair had taken part in. They had struck up a friendship during the three months they had spent together, and Blair had since heard that Herb was now working as a ramrod.

The five riders stopped as they reached Blair and Norton.

'Howdy, Herb,' said Blair.

'Howdy, Blair,' responded his friend, a cheerful-looking character with a shock of red hair. 'I heard before I left Texas that you were due to take a herd up to Wyoming Territory. So I'm mighty curious when I find you here, well off the Western trail, and pretty short-handed, to say the least.'

'It's a long story,' said Blair. 'I'll tell it to you over a drink of coffee. Light down, all of you.'

Later, when Blair had finished talking to an audience which listened with rapt attention, Myers spoke.

'We've just delivered a herd to Dakota Territory,' he said, 'and we were warned when we were in Kansas, to watch out for the Mulvaney gang. There's a lot of ranchers in these parts who'll be mighty grateful to you for breaking the gang up like you've just done.'

'You can see I'm in a fix,' said Blair. 'I've got to get this herd to a ranch twenty miles north-east of Cheyenne. It's a job the two of us can't handle. I'm wondering if you men would help out, if you've got the time to spare. I figure it would take us about twenty-one days to get there.

'I'm willing to pay you twice the ordinary rate,' Blair went on, 'I'm sure there won't be no argument from the owner about that.'

'We've got a bit of time to spare,' said Myers, 'and I figure we can help you out if the others agree. But there ain't no need to pay any double rate. We sure don't want to profit from what the Mulvaney gang did to you.'

He consulted with his men, who all agreed to help drive the herd into Wyoming. Then he walked over to Blair.

'We're all with you,' he said. 'It sure was

lucky for you we happened to be riding back this way. When do we start?'

'The herd's been grazing this morning,' said Blair, 'so I figure we can drive the cattle a few miles this afternoon, after we've had some dinner. There's plenty of food in the chuck wagon to last us a while. Have you got a cook with you?'

'Sure,' said Myers, 'and a good one. I'll get him to whip up a meal for us.'

Twenty days later, they handed over the herd, in good condition, at the Bar 10 Ranch in Wyoming, in exchange for a previously agreed sum handed over by the buyer. Blair sold the chuck wagon and the spare saddle horses in Cheyenne, and using a letter of credit on a Cheyenne bank he handed each man his pay and arranged with the bank for the proceeds of the sale to be transferred to the seller in Texas.

The following morning Blair thanked Myers and his men as they prepared to leave for Texas. Their intention was to join a Union Pacific train at the rail depot in

Cheyenne and make the long journey home by rail. Then Blair spoke to Norton, who had decided to accompany Myers and the others.

'Tell Tex Gardner exactly what happened to the trail hands and the herd,' he said, 'and say that I'm going after Mulvaney and that I'm hoping I'll be back in Texas in time for the spring roundups. The only clue I have up to now is that I think Mulvaney was going to hand over the herd to a man called Hiram Trent. I've checked with Herb Myers in case he'd heard of this Trent, but he said he hadn't. I'm going to keep on riding in the same direction as Mulvaney did after I plugged him.'

Blair left Cheyenne shortly after Myers and the others, and headed for the place where he had put paid to five members of the Mulvaney gang. When he arrived there four days later, he camped for the night, and on the following morning he set off in the direction taken by Mulvaney after he had been shot. He had little hope of following the tracks, made just under four weeks earlier, of the outlaw's horse, but somebody might remember seeing a wounded man around at the time.

In the early afternoon he rode into the head of a shallow valley, narrow at that point, and spotted a single homestead on the opposite bank of the river running through the valley. He crossed the river and rode towards a man working in one of the fields. He was a worried-looking man, middle-aged, and moving slowly, and as Blair drew closer he could see a pallor on the man's face as if he was recovering from some severe illness. He stopped in front of the homesteader, who had turned to face him.

'Howdy,' said Blair.

'Howdy,' said the settler.

'I'm hoping maybe you can help me,' said Blair. 'My name's Calhoun. I work as a trail boss. I'm on the trail of a rustler called Mulvaney whose gang killed seven of my men west of here. I know I wounded him, and the last tracks I saw of his horse were heading this way.' He described Mulvaney, then continued. 'He may have passed through here about four weeks ago. Did you happen to see him?'

'My name's Mariner,' said the homesteader. 'I didn't see this man Mulvaney but from what you tell me it's possible he was here about four weeks ago. Somebody took my saddle horse in the night and left a lame one behind.'

'Is the horse here?' asked Blair. He remembered the mount on which Mulvaney had escaped. It was a chestnut, with a distinctive white blaze on the forehead.

'It is,' replied Mariner. 'It was all right after a few days' rest. It's a good horse. I reckon I got the best of the deal.'

'D'you mind if I take a look at it?' asked Blair.

'Help yourself,' said Mariner. 'It's over there.' He pointed towards a small pasture near the house.

Blair rode over and inspected the animal.

He was sure he was looking at the horse the wounded Mulvaney had been riding. He rode back to Mariner and thanked the homesteader for his help. He asked him if there was a doctor anywhere nearby.

'Five miles east,' said Mariner, 'in a town called Winthrop, by the river. You'll find Doc Barclay there. He's a good man.'

'Does the name Hiram Trent mean anything to you?' asked Blair as he was leaving.

Mariner shook his head. 'Never heard that name before,' he said. As Blair rode off, Mariner looked after him for a while, then slowly resumed his labours.

As Blair headed for Winthrop, he could see grazing cattle ahead of him where the valley widened. After riding about two miles, he rounded a small hill and saw, some way ahead of him, a stationary buckboard with no horses hitched to it. Beyond the buckboard were two distant riders, heading east, and to the north Blair could see two horses grazing. A figure was lying on the ground near the buckboard.

Riding fast, Blair reached the vehicle and dismounted. The figure on the ground was that of a young woman in her early twenties, slim and tanned, with blonde hair partially covering her face. Blair bent over her, moved the hair aside, and saw that on the side of her face was a nasty cut from which blood was flowing. As he examined the wound, her eyes opened and she shrank away from him.

'It's all right,' he said. 'I'm here to help. Just happened on you by chance.'

He took off his bandanna and handed it to her. 'You've got a bad cut on your face,' he said. 'Make a pad of that bandanna and hold it against the cut.'

When she had done this he asked her if the two grazing horses nearby were her draft horses. She nodded, as she got to her feet with Blair's help.

'I'll round them up and get them hitched,' said Blair, 'then we'll get you to the doctor in Winthrop as quick as we can.'

He helped her up on to the buckboard seat, then rode off to collect the two horses. When he had hitched them to the buckboard, he tied his own horse behind, climbed on to the seat beside her, and took hold of the reins. Stealing a glance at her, it struck him that it was a long time since he had seen such an attractive woman.

On the way into Winthrop she told Blair what had happened. She was on her way into town to get some provisions from the store, when two hands called Price and Pardee from the STU Ranch which stretched down the valley, had ridden up and stopped her. They had unhitched the horses and chased them off, and when she tried to stop them doing this, Pardee had struck her hard on the face and had left her lying unconscious on the ground.

'Have you any idea why they did this?' asked Blair.

'The STU is owned by a man called Jason Kilby,' she said. 'His foreman has made it clear that Kilby don't want us around here, and he's told my father, who runs a homestead a few miles back, that he's got to leave. But Father's a stubborn man. He knows we have a legal right to stay where we are and he says he's not moving. I guess Kilby's getting impatient.'

'Your father's name wouldn't be Mariner, would it?' asked Blair. 'If it is, I spoke to him a short while ago.'

'Yes, it is,' she replied. 'Grant Mariner. I'm Mary Mariner.'

'Blair Calhoun,' said Blair. 'Your father didn't look too spry when I was talking to him.'

'We've had a bad time lately,' she said. 'About six weeks ago my mother and father both went down with diphtheria. Mother died, but Father pulled through.' She wiped a tear from her eye, then continued. 'He's been grieving for her and he's still weak from the sickness. Doc Barclay says it'll be a while before he gets all his strength back.'

Blair explained to Mary how he came to be in the area, then they sat in silence for a while as they drove into the one and only street in Winthrop.

'Doc Barclay's house is on the other side of town,' said Mary, 'On the right.'

As they drove through the town, Blair saw Mary staring at two horses tied to a hitching rail outside a saloon. One was a pinto, the other a chestnut.

'Are those the horses ridden by the men who stopped you?' he asked.

She nodded. 'Yes,' she replied, 'they're the ones. Pardee was riding the chestnut.'

Moments later, they stopped outside the doctor's house, and found him at home. He greeted Mary and ushered them inside. He examined the cut on her face. The flesh around the cut and around her left eye was badly discoloured.

'There's one good thing, Mary,' he said, as he deftly cleaned the wound and fastened a pad over it. 'This cut don't need stitching, and when it's healed up it won't leave much of a mark behind. But how in tarnation did you come by it?'

'It was Pardee and Price,' she told him. 'They stopped me when I was driving the buckboard into town, and unhitched the horses. Mr Calhoun here happened along later and helped me get into town.'

Barclay cursed under his breath. 'Kilby's going too far,' he said. 'He has no right to harass you like this. Just because we ain't got no lawman nearby, he thinks he can do as he wants. Or maybe I should say that it's his foreman, Munro, who thinks he can do as he wants.

'About two months ago,' he explained to Blair. 'Kilby's wife died of pneumonia. Up to then he and his wife had been very friendly with Mary and her parents, and with me as well. But when Kilby lost his wife, it seems like he went to pieces, and he ain't been in town since she was buried.

'We heard,' he went on, 'that just after the funeral a stranger called Munro turned up at the STU and asked for a job. Just how he persuaded Kilby to take him on, I don't know, but he got a job as foreman. Soon after he came, he brought in Pardee and Price and three other hands, all tough-looking characters, and fired the men who were there when he started to work for Kilby. Munro turned out to be a hard man, set on forcing Mary and her father off their homestead.

'Kilby still lives on the ranch,' he continued, 'but it seems that he leaves the running of it to Munro. I went out to see him once, but Munro said he didn't want to see anybody.'

'The same thing happened to my father,' said Mary.

'And Munro is stepping up the pressure on Miss Mariner and her father,' said Blair. 'That accounts for today's incident?'

'That's right,' said Barclay.

'Are there any other settlers in the valley?' asked Blair.

'Yes,' replied Barclay, 'six more families, but they're all well down the valley, east of town.'

'Has Munro been pressuring them to

leave as well?' asked Blair.

'Not yet,' replied Barclay. 'I wondered about that. Then I figured maybe he'd decided to deal with them one at a time.'

'What I'm going to do now,' said Blair, 'is see Miss Mariner back to the homestead. That was a nasty knock she took, and I figure she don't feel much like driving that buckboard.'

'I'd be obliged,' she said, 'if you've got the time. But first, I have to call at the store.'

'That's fine,' said Blair. 'While you're in there, there's some business I have to attend to myself.'

He turned to the doctor. 'You might have some information that could be useful to me,' he said, and went on to tell Barclay of the rustling of his herd and of Mulvaney's escape. He asked him whether a wounded man had visited him around four weeks ago.

'He sure did,' replied Barclay, 'in the middle of the night. And he held a gun on me all the time I was tending him.'

Blair described Mulvaney. 'That was him

all right,' said the doctor.

'Was he hurt bad?' asked Blair.

'Bad enough,' replied Barclay. 'There was a bullet lodged in his side and a bullet-graze on his arm. I got the bullet out. It hadn't done any serious damage as far as I could see. I bandaged him up and he left.'

'So you reckon he'll pull through all right?' said Blair.

'Don't see why not,' replied the doctor, 'if he has the sense to take things easy for a spell. You figuring to catch up with him?'

'Yes,' said Blair, grimly. 'I have a big score to settle with Mulvaney. By the way,' he went on, 'have you ever heard of a Hiram Trent in these parts?'

'Can't say I have,' said Barclay. 'No, I'm sure I haven't.'

Blair helped Mary on to the buckboard, then went back to the doctor for a moment, to get a description of Price and Pardee. Barclay obliged, and warned him that Price fancied himself as a gunfighter. Returning to the buckboard, Blair drove back along the street to the general store, and arranged to meet Mary there when she had finished her purchases. When she had gone inside, Blair walked further along the street to the saloon. The chestnut and pinto were still standing at the hitching rail outside.

Blair checked his Peacemaker, pushed the swing doors open, and walked into the saloon. He paused just inside, and looked around. Price and Pardee were standing together at the bar. The three other customers, townspeople by the look of them, were sitting at a table well back from the bar, against a wall. The barkeep was standing close to the two STU hands, on the other side of the bar.

Price was a short, thin, weasel-faced man, wearing a right-hand gun in a tied-down holster. Pardee was around average height, stocky and bearded, with a coarse, brutal face. He, also, was armed.

The two men looked at Blair as he walked up to the bar and turned to face them from a distance of six feet or so.

'I'm looking,' said Blair in a loud voice, and addressing nobody in particular, 'for a couple of bullies from the STU called Price and Pardee who assaulted the daughter of a nester outside of town not more than two hours ago. They unhitched the horses from her buckboard and left her stranded out there. And the one called Pardee punched her on the face and knocked her out.'

The barkeep and the three men at the table all stared at the two STU hands.

Pardee, crimson with rage, spoke. 'You've found the men you're looking for,' he said, 'and let me tell you that what we do around here is no business of yours. Strangers ain't welcome here. I'm telling you to ride on and don't come back.'

'But I figure it is my business,' said Blair, 'when a defenceless woman's treated like Mary Mariner was.'

Pardee spoke to Price, without turning his head. 'You'd better deal with this, Bob,' he said. 'This man needs to be shown that the STU runs things around here, and he ain't welcome, interfering like this. What he just said about us was real insulting. I reckon it's a shooting matter, don't you?'

Price, his thin lips twisted in a sneer, observed Blair malevolently. He was, he thought, really going to enjoy gunning this man down. It was a while since he'd had a human target to practise on. Smoothly, he drew his gun, with the same speed and precision which had served him so well in the past, but the shouted command 'Hold it!' from Blair, and the sight of Blair's cocked gun already pointing at his chest, froze his own movement just after his gun had cleared the holster.

Badly shaken by the experience of being so comprehensively outgunned, Price glared at Blair and remained motionless. Pardee, open-mouthed at his side, did the same. The other three customers and the barkeep knew that they had witnessed a show of gunfighting expertise considerably above the average. They awaited Blair's next move with interest.

'I could've shot you both down,' said Blair, 'but after what you did to that young woman I felt I wanted to get my hands on you.

'You, Price,' he went on, 'take hold of that gun of yours by the barrel, easy-like, and throw it down on the floor on the other side of the bar.'

As Price hesitated, Blair sent a bullet into the floor half an inch from the toe of the STU hand's left boot. Hastily, Price threw his gun over the bar and a moment later, at Blair's command, Pardee did likewise.

'Now,' said Blair, 'I reckon I can take you both on at the same time. I don't figure Price is much of a fighter without a gun in his hand. And you, Pardee, maybe you're pretty good at beating up women, but I reckon you'd soon turn yellow if you had a real fight on your hands.'

He holstered the Peacemaker. 'I don't aim to use this gun,' he said. 'I'm waiting.'

He stood, seemingly relaxed, a little way out from the bar, facing the two STU hands. Incensed, the two men rushed at him together. At the last moment, with a nimbleness of foot which surprised his opponents, he darted out of their path, turned, and came up behind them. He gave Pardee a violent push in the back which caused him to lose his balance, crash into the wall of the saloon, and fall heavily to the floor.

Then, immediately, Blair caught Price by the back of his collar with one hand and by his belt with the other. He hoisted the STU hand off the floor, ran towards the window, and launched him through it head first. Price landed on the boardwalk outside amid a shower of broken glass and timber, and lay there, stunned.

Blair turned and walked towards Pardee, who had risen to his feet, breathing heavily, his face flushed with rage. Once again the ranch hand launched himself at Blair, his fists flailing. Once again Blair sidestepped from in front of his opponent and as Pardee blundered past him, he put all his weight behind a solid right-hand punch high on his opponent's cheekbone. Pardee cannoned into the bar and dropped to the floor, blood flowing from a cut under his left eye.

Blair waited while Pardee got to his feet and turned to face him. The ranch hand came towards him, more cautiously this time. Blair stood his ground, blocked two wild punches from Pardee, then sank his right fist deep into the pit of his opponent's stomach. Pardee doubled up in agony, then, as he tried to straighten up, Blair repeated the punch and followed up with a right hook to the ranch hand's jaw. Pardee, doubled up, collapsed on the floor and showed no inclination to continue the fight.

As Blair stepped away from his victim, a movement at the saloon doors caught his attention. A rifle barrel had appeared over the top of the door and behind the barrel he could see Price's head, with the blood streaming down his face. He guessed that the STU hand had probably taken the rifle from the saddle holster on his horse.

Price swung the rifle barrel round to draw a bead on Blair, and his finger tightened on the trigger just as Blair put a bullet through his head. The bullet from the rifle buried itself harmlessly in the ceiling of the saloon. As Price fell, his body pushed the doors open and he lay half in, and half out of, the saloon.

Blair looked over at Pardee, who was lying on the floor with his back arched, and his hands clutching at his stomach. His eyes were open. Blair continued to watch in silence as the ranch hand first sat up, then slowly rose to his feet. Sullenly, he faced Blair, the blood still running down his face from the cut under his eye.

'What I want you to do now, Pardee,' said Blair, 'is to take Price back to the STU and tell Kilby and Munro that Mariner ain't got no intention of leaving his homestead, and that I'm here to see that nobody tries to change his mind for him by playing any more dirty tricks like the one you played today.

'Let's go,' he said. 'I figure you ain't in no shape now to lay Price across his horse's back, so I'll do it for you.'

Pardee walked unsteadily out of the saloon, stepping over his partner's body, and slowly and painfully he mounted his horse. Blair dragged Price's body over to the pinto and laid him across its back, then handed the reins to Pardee. He, and the small crowd of onlookers attracted by the shooting, watched as the two horses walked slowly out of town. Mary Mariner, the storekeeper by her side, observed the scene from the boardwalk outside the store.

Blair walked back into the saloon and spoke to the bartender.

'I'm mighty sorry about that busted window,' he said, 'but you could see that I had to find some way of splitting those two up. I'm figuring to be around here for a spell. Just let me have the bill for the repairs, will you?'

The bartender nodded, and Blair walked out of the saloon and over to Mary outside the store. He saw that her purchases had been loaded on to the buckboard, and guessed she was ready to leave. His horse was still tied behind the vehicle.

'Ready to go?' he asked.

'I'm ready,' she replied. 'What happened inside the saloon?'

'Well,' replied Blair. 'After what Pardee and Price did to you, I figured they needed a lesson in manners, so that's just what I gave them. Price made the mistake of trying to shoot me down with his rifle.'

She looked worried. 'What's Munro going to do to you when he hears about this?' she asked. 'Don't you think you'd better ride away from here right now?'

'Not a chance,' said Blair, smiling at her. 'I'm looking forward to meeting Munro, and on top of that I don't want to leave when I've only just met you.'

He helped her on to the buckboard seat, climbed up after her, and they headed for the homestead.

# EIGHT

When Blair and Mary reached the homestead, her father was surprised to see Blair again. Mary explained what had happened and Mariner thanked Blair for his help.

'I just can't figure out,' he said, 'why Jason Kilby's letting all this happen. I always figured him for a decent man and a good friend.'

'I can see you ain't got all your strength back yet from that illness your daughter was telling me about,' said Blair. 'If you ain't got no objection I'd like to stay on here a while in case Munro starts to hassle you again. And maybe you could do with a helping hand around the homestead for a while.'

Mary and her father both stared at Blair. The relief on their faces was evident.

'I can't deny,' said Mariner, 'that I'll feel a

whole lot better if you're around. But this ain't your fight. And what about that murdering rustler you're chasing?'

'Mulvaney can wait,' replied Blair. 'As soon as we've dealt with Munro and Kilby I'll get on his trail again.'

'In that case,' said Mariner, 'we'd sure appreciate your help. We've got a spare room here you can sleep in. Mary'll fix it up in no time.'

The two men continued talking while Mary was seeing to the room.

'Mary and me've had a bad time since my wife Emily died,' he said, 'and we're never going to forget her, but I think maybe I'm perking up a little at last. What still worries me, though,' he went on, 'is Mary. It'll be no life for her, living alone with me. She should be married, in a place of her own.

'She's had plenty of offers, of course,' he continued, 'but she reckons she just ain't met the right man yet. When she does, she says she'll know it right away. Meantime, as you can guess, I sure am glad to have her

115

around. She's been a good daughter to both of us.'

He paused, then continued. 'What's your plan of campaign?' he asked.

'There's something odd about this whole business,' said Blair. 'Why hasn't Kilby been seen by anybody outside the ranch since his wife's funeral? Why did Munro replace the STU ranch hands with his own men? Why are you the only homesteaders they've threatened up to now?

'I think,' he went on, 'that maybe I can get some answers to these questions if I ride out to the STU after dark and have a good look round. I'll take my field glasses with me. Have you ever been out there yourself?'

'The three of us used to go out there regular before Jason Kilby's wife died,' said Mariner.

Blair asked him to describe the layout of the ranch buildings and the interior layout of the ranch house. When the settler had done this, Blair asked him to describe Kilby and Munro.

'You couldn't mistake Kilby if you saw him,' said Mariner. 'He's only around five foot three tall, and very stout. And he's got a bad limp. He damaged a leg a few years back, and it gives way sometimes. As for Munro, he's about your height, I'd say, but a lot slimmer, with light brown hair, and clean-shaven. And he's got a scar on his cheek.'

Blair decided to ride to the STU during the night, so as to arrive just before daybreak, at some high ground which Mariner had described to him, from which, unobserved, he could look down on the ranch buildings during the day.

They all had a meal, then Blair slept until it was time for him to leave. Mary and her father got up to see him off, and Mary handed him some food to take with him. He told them he couldn't be sure when he'd be back.

'I'm worried,' said Mary, 'that maybe we won't see you again. You'll be up against four STU hands out there, as well as

Munro. Maybe it's too big a risk for you to take for us.'

'I'll be all right,' smiled Blair. 'I don't aim to tackle them all at once. See you later.'

They watched as he faded into the darkness.

'That's a brave man,' said Mariner. 'We're lucky he turned up just now. I've seen the way you look at him, Mary,' he went on, 'and I got the idea that maybe the right man for you has come along at last.'

'He has,' said Mary. 'I know it. But am I the right woman for him?'

'He'd be a fool to think different,' said her father.

'We'll see,' said Mary, and went back to bed. She did not sleep for the rest of the night.

When Blair reached the vantage point described by Mariner, it was half an hour before daybreak. He was on the top of the slope on the north side of the valley. He tied his horse behind a large boulder and waited for daylight.

When it came, he could see the ranch buildings on the valley floor, about half a mile distant. Cattle were grazing along the valley in both directions. From cover, Blair kept the ranch buildings under observation through the field glasses. It wasn't long before four men came out of what he took to be the bunkhouse, and went into a small building, probably the cookshack, close by.

Shortly after this a man came out of the two-storey house and went into the cookshack. From his size, Blair figured that this could be Munro. The same man came out a few minutes later and carried something into the house. Then he returned to the cookshack and stayed there until half an hour later, when he came out with the four men who had gone in earlier.

Two of the men saddled up and rode off, one up the valley, the other down, and quickly disappeared from Blair's view. The man he took to be Munro went inside the house and the other two went into the barn. Throughout the day Blair saw the three men moving around and in the afternoon he observed the return of the two hands who had ridden off earlier. Of Kilby, there had been no sign, but Blair had received the impression that Munro was living in the house and that food and drink were being carried in there for someone else. This could mean that Kilby was inside, confined there for some reason.

After dark, Blair had a meal, then rested until an hour after midnight, when he rode down towards the ranch buildings. Leaving his horse tied to the pasture fence, he continued on foot towards the house, carrying two short lengths of rope over his shoulder. No lights were showing inside.

He paused outside the door of the house and listened for a moment before trying it. It was not locked. Cautiously, he pushed it open and stepped inside. He struck a match and lit a small oil lamp on a table close by. Turning the flame down low, he walked towards the foot of the stairs Mariner had described to him and slowly climbed them.

At the top of the stairs a narrow passage led to two bedroom doors, both closed. The first one Blair came to was locked from the outside, the key remaining in the lock, and it was further secured by a stout bolt which had been pushed into a hole in the door frame. Blair now had more than a strong suspicion that Kilby was a prisoner inside the room.

He walked along to the door of the second bedroom and stood outside it, listening. He heard a faint snore coming from inside the room. He walked back to the door of the first bedroom, turned the key in the lock and slowly pulled back the bolt. Then he opened the door just sufficiently to allow him to slip into the room, and closed it behind him. He drew his gun and looked across at the bed against the far wall. A man was lying on it, his face turned to the wall. The outline under the bedclothes showed that he was a short man of stout build.

Blair walked over to the bed and put the lamp down on a bedside table, turning it up a little as he did so. He holstered his gun, then picked up a folded towel from a chair, and as the man turned on to his back, he slapped the towel across his mouth and held it firmly in position. The man's eyes flicked open and he looked up into Blair's face. He started to struggle.

'I'm a friend of the Mariners,' whispered Blair, urgently. 'I'm here to help you. You going to keep quiet?'

The man stopped struggling and nodded. Blair removed the towel.

'You're Jason Kilby?' he asked.

The man nodded, then spoke. 'Munro and his men have been keeping me here against my will,' he said. 'Can you get me away? I'll tell you all about it later. Just now, I want to get somewhere safe.'

'That's where I'm figuring to take you,' said Blair, 'and while I'm here I aim to capture Munro and take him along with us. Is that him in the next room?'

'That's him,' said Kilby. 'All the others are in the bunkhouse.'

'Are you with me, then?' asked Blair.

'I'm with you,' replied Kilby. 'That Munro is a devil. I can't wait to see him in the hands of the law.'

'I'll get him to the law,' said Blair, and waited while Kilby dressed. Then, handing the lamp to Kilby and telling the rancher to follow right behind him, Blair left the bedroom and walked up to the door of the room in which Munro was sleeping. He flung it open and ran across to the bed. Munro, jerking into wakefulness, raised his head and his hand reached out towards the six-gun on the bedside table.

Blair lifted his Peacemaker and slammed the barrel along the side of Munro's head, knocking him senseless. Hurriedly, Blair and Kilby dressed their victim, then Blair tied his hands and feet, and gagged him with a piece torn from one of the sheets. Handing Munro's gun to Kilby, Blair slung the unconscious man over his shoulder, and, with Kilby following behind, he walked over to the place where he had left his horse, and dropped Munro, who was beginning to show signs of coming round, on to the ground. He turned to Kilby.

'We need two horses,' he said, 'and a saddle and two bridles. And some more rope as well.'

'I know exactly where I can get all those things,' said Kilby. 'They're in a shed next to the barn. You wait here. When I get back, we can get a couple of mounts from the pasture. They're all broke-in there.'

Half an hour later, they had slung Munro over the back of a horse and had tied him securely on. He was now fully conscious and mouthing threats and curses under the gag. Blair and Kilby mounted, and Blair took the reins of Munro's mount. They headed for the Mariner homestead.

When they arrived there, the sun was just lifting over the high ground to the east. They rode up to the house, and Blair called out and waited until Mariner and Mary appeared in the doorway. They stared in disbelief at the sight of the two men with him. Kilby and Blair dismounted, untied Munro from his mount and pulled him off its back, to sit on the ground in front of them. Blair untied the rope around his ankles.

'Can I take him in the barn and tie him up there?' he asked. 'Then we'll tell you what happened.'

'Sure,' said Grant Mariner. 'There's some more rope in there if you need it.'

Blair pulled Munro to his feet and prodded him in the back with his Peacemaker, as the prisoner headed for the barn. Inside, in the middle of the floor, was a vertical post supporting the loft, and they decided to tie Munro to this post, in a sitting position, for the time being. Blair ordered him to sit down against it.

Kilby limped towards a length of rope hanging on the wall, but as he passed the prisoner his bad leg suddenly gave way beneath him and he lurched sideways and fell down against Munro. Twisting his hands round inside the rope binding them loosely together. Munro grabbed the handle of his own six-gun, which Kilby had pushed under his belt, and pulled it out. Frantically, he cocked it and brought it round to bear on Blair, but he dropped it without firing as the bullet from Blair's Peacemaker drilled into his chest. He died seconds later.

Hearing the gunshot, Mary and her father ran into the barn. They stared at the body on the floor and the gun lying beside it.

'Munro grabbed the gun Mr Kilby was carrying,' explained Blair. 'It was a close call.'

Leaving Munro in the barn, they went into the house, where Kilby told them what had happened since the death of his wife. He said he had taken Munro on and had given him a free hand, because he didn't feel like running the spread himself at the time. But as soon as Munro had brought his own men in, the rancher had found that he was a prisoner on his own spread. He was locked in his bedroom all the time, and food and drink were brought to him there. Now and again he was forced to sign a paper authorizing Munro to collect from the bank in Winthrop the amount of cash which would normally be required to run the ranch.

It wasn't long, Kilby told his listeners, before he discovered what Munro was up to. His intention was to gradually drive cattle off the ranch, taking them through the head of the valley. They would take, say, a hundred head at a time, and hand them over to accomplices outside the valley, who would drive them to a buyer not too far away.

'That explains it,' said Blair.

'Explains what?' asked Kilby.

'It explains,' replied Blair, 'why Munro was so set on forcing Mr Mariner and his daughter off their homestead. It's the only homestead anywhere near the head of the valley, and Munro was planning to drive the stolen cattle right past it. If it was occupied, he knew that the settler living there couldn't help but see those cattle being driven out of the valley, a hundred or so at a time, and people would start asking questions.'

'One thing I didn't know, Grant,' said Kilby, 'was that you and Mary had been threatened by Munro. I'm sorry about that. I'm sure what Mr Calhoun says is right.'

He turned to Blair. 'I sure am obliged to you for what you've done,' he said. 'I don't think that Munro meant to leave me alive when he'd finished stealing my cattle. What d'you reckon we should do about the men on the STU?'

'I've got a feeling,' said Blair, 'that when Pardee and the others find that you and Munro are missing, they'll know that the game is up, and they won't waste no time in leaving the STU.'

Blair, Mariner, Kilby and four homesteaders from down the valley, who had offered to join the party, rode to the STU Ranch in the afternoon. All were armed. The ranch buildings were deserted and there were signs of a hurried departure.

'I reckon you've seen the last of them,' said Blair. 'How are you going to run the place?'

'I have an old friend who owns a big ranch not far south of here,' said Kilby. 'I'm going to get in touch with him right away. I'll ask him to lend me a few hands until I can recruit a new outfit. And I know a couple of men in town who'll help me out meantime.'

Leaving Kilby behind, the settlers rode back to their homesteads. Blair rode back with Mariner. With relief, Mary saw the two men riding up the valley towards the house. Later, over supper, Mariner asked Blair how he planned to catch up with Mulvaney.

'I'm heading north-east,' said Blair, 'because he was heading that way when he passed through here. As I go along I'll ask people if they've seen or heard of him, and maybe I'll be lucky. Would you like me to stay on here for a few more days to help you out?'

'Thanks for the offer,' said Mariner, 'but I'm feeling a lot better now and I reckon we can manage. The sooner you get on Mulvaney's trail, the more likely you are to catch up with him.'

'I'll leave in the morning then,' said Blair.

Shortly after this, the tired homesteader excused himself and went to his bedroom. Mary cleared up after the meal, then sat down in the living-room with Blair.

'Will we ever see you around here again, I wonder?' she asked.

'I reckon it's up to you,' replied Blair, smiling. 'It all depends on whether, after all this time, you reckon you've met the right man at last.'

She blushed. 'I can see Pa's been talking about me,' she said. 'Maybe you think it's a bit forward, me saying this, but there ain't no doubt in my mind that the right man *has* come along. But like I said to Pa, am I the right woman for him?'

'There ain't no doubt about that, either,' said Blair. 'I've knowed it ever since I took you to the doctor in Winthrop. I'll be coming to court you just as soon as I've settled with Mulvaney.'

'I'll be waiting,' she said. 'I can see that chasing Mulvaney is something you've got to do.'

# NINE

Blair took his leave of Mary and her father, and rode in the same direction, north-easterly, in which Mulvaney had been driving the stolen herd. Enquiries made of the few people he met during the day, concerning Mulvaney and Hiram Trent, were fruitless.

He camped out overnight and on the following morning he was crossing what looked like a fair-sized ranch, well-stocked with cattle, when he spotted a group of people in the distance, close to a line of trees fringing a small stream.

He rode towards them and as he drew closer he saw a group of men who looked like ranch hands, standing by an individual wearing a Montana Peak hat with a high crown, who looked like he was in charge of them. This man was Will Murray, owner of the Lazy M Ranch over which Blair was riding. Next to him stood his foreman, Calvert.

One of the hands was holding the reins of a horse, against which was standing a man whose hands were bound, and around whose neck a noose had been placed. The end of the rope had been thrown over the branch of a cottonwood tree, directly over the prisoner, a small man, roughly-dressed, with a look of desperation on his face. Facing the group, a few yards away, was an elderly man in his sixties, slim and grey-haired. Pinned to his vest was the badge of a county sheriff.

As Blair came to a stop close to the group, which numbered eight men including the prisoner, Murray spoke to him. 'Ride on, stranger,' he said. 'This is no concern of yours.'

Blair dismounted and dropped his horse's reins. 'I think I'll stay around a little while,' he said. 'I'm a curious sort of a fellow and it looks like there's an interesting situation developing here. I'd like to see what happens.'

Murray glared at Blair, but before he could reply to him the sheriff spoke.

'I'll tell you again, Murray,' he said. 'Lynching is against the law. You have no right to hang Mullery here. Hand him over to me and if I find proof that he's been rustling, the law will deal with him. As far as I can make out, you found Mullery riding across your range, but he wasn't driving any of your cows off at the time.'

'Catching him on my range was enough for me,' said Murray, grimly. 'Everybody knows he takes a few beeves whenever he feels like it. And horses too.'

'There's no law that says a man can't ride over your range, Murray,' said the sheriff. 'Hand Mullery over to me and I'll be on my way.'

'You've been a bit of a nuisance to me lately, Blaney,' said Murray, who was a stocky man of average height, in his fifties, with a hard eye and a ruthless face. 'I reckon you're too old for the job,' he went on. 'Maybe you were pretty handy with a gun in the old days, but I reckon any one of my men here could outgun you nowadays. Why don't you let a younger man take over? Maybe we'd get a bit more protection then from men like Mullery here.'

Blaney's face reddened and he glanced at Blair, who walked over and stood by his side, facing Murray and his men.

'I'm telling you again, Murray,' said Blaney. 'Hand Mullery over to me and let us leave.'

Murray glared at Blair. 'I've warned you stranger,' he said. 'Interfere in this affair and you're liable to end up dead.' Then he replied to Blaney.

'Mullery's going to hang,' he said, 'whatever you and that interfering busybody with you think about it. You're going to be in real trouble if you interfere.'

Murray's men watched the sheriff closely,

awaiting his next move, and ready to open fire if Murray gave the order. Blair's move was totally unexpected by them. With eye-defeating rapidity he lifted the Peacemaker out of its holster and sent a bullet through the high crown of Murray's hat, which jerked off his head and fell to the ground. The whole group jumped, including the prisoner.

The sheriff's gun was out fractionally after Blair's, and before the startled hands could bring their weapons up, they found themselves facing two six-guns in the hands of two determined and capable gun-handlers.

'Maybe you've noticed, Murray,' said Blair, 'that my gun's pointed right at your belly. If any of your men makes a wrong move, that's where I'm going to put a bullet.'

Still closely watching the hands, Blair spoke to the sheriff.

'This is your show, Sheriff,' he said. 'You give the orders and I'll keep an eye on

Murray and the others.'

The sheriff nodded, and ordered the rancher and his men to throw their weapons on the ground near him. Then he told one of the men to release Mullery, who then came over to stand beside Blair.

'I'm taking your horses and weapons, Murray,' said Blaney. 'I'll leave them a couple of miles from here. As for the threats you just made against myself and Mullery, and the man who just perforated your headgear, I'm going to speak to Judge Hall about it the next time he comes into town. When I've seen him, maybe I'll be back here to arrest you.'

'You'd better bring plenty of men,' blustered Murray. 'You won't take me without a fight.'

'You talk like a fool, Murray,' said the sheriff. 'If it's necessary, I'll get the army to help me out. Maybe, one day, you'll realize that nobody is above the law.'

As the three men rode off, leaving the fuming Murray and his men behind them,

Blaney spoke to Blair. 'I'm sure obliged to you, stranger,' he said. 'You got a name?'

'Blair Calhoun,' said Blair. 'I was glad to help. I was a lawman myself for a spell, in south Texas.'

'That's a mighty fast draw you've got,' observed Blaney. 'Faster than I could manage, even in my prime. It's lucky you were there. I think Murray meant it when he threatened us.'

'I think you're right,' said Blair. 'Where are we heading now?'

'I've got an office in Fairborn, ten miles east of here,' replied Blaney. 'You want to come along?'

'Might as well,' said Blair. 'I'll stay overnight.'

A mile and a half further on, they left behind the horses and guns belonging to Murray and his men and continued on their way. Mullery rode up alongside Blair.

'I sure thought I was a goner there, mister,' he said. 'I figure you saved my hide. It's pretty scandalous when an innocent man can't go for a ride without getting strung up.'

'Take no notice of him, Calhoun,' said the sheriff. 'I know that Mullery has a weakness for stealing cattle and horses. He don't operate in a big way. Just takes a few at a time. Trouble is, I've never been able to pin anything on him so far. But I figure he'll get caught in the end. He was lucky we were both there today.'

'You shouldn't ought to blacken my character like that, Sheriff,' said Mullery indignantly. 'What're you going to do with me?'

'I'm going to slap you into a cell,' replied Blaney, 'while I try to find out what you were doing riding across Lazy M range.'

When they reached Fairborn, the sheriff put Mullery into one of the cells behind his office, then he and Blair went into the restaurant next door for supper. Over the meal, Blair told Blaney about his quest for Mulvaney and the reason for it. The sheriff regarded him with interest.

'So you're the man,' he said, 'who pretty near wiped out the Mulvaney gang single-handed. I heard about it only yesterday. There's a lot of folks who're going to be mighty grateful to you when they hear about it. They were all wanted men in Dakota Territory and Kansas.

'It's just struck me,' he went on. 'There should be some reward money due to you for what you did to the Mulvaney gang. I'll make some enquiries for you. Will you call back here when you've dealt with Mulvaney?'

'I'll do that,' said Blair. 'Come to think of it, that money sure could be useful. As for dealing with Mulvaney,' he went on, 'maybe you can help me. When he was holding me prisoner, I overheard him say that he was going to hand the herd over to a man called Hiram Trent. Does that name mean anything to you?'

The sheriff's brow furrowed and his eyes half closed, as he thought long and hard.

'I'm sure I've heard that name before,' he

said, then paused for a moment. 'Yes, I remember now,' he went on. 'Trent runs a ranch about fifty miles north-east of here, outside of my jurisdiction. About two months ago a small herd passed here on the way from Colorado to the Circle T Ranch, that's Trent's spread. The ramrod told me where they were heading. I'm pretty sure that this particular deal was a legitimate one. I'd met the ramrod before.'

'Thanks for the information,' said Blair. 'Tomorrow morning I'll head for the Circle T. It looks like Trent was due to receive stolen cattle from Mulvaney, and I guess that when I got the herd back, Mulvaney figured he'd better let Trent know what had happened.'

'I guess you're right,' said the sheriff, 'but likely he's left there by now.'

'Yes,' agreed Blair, 'but maybe I can find out where he went. I don't suppose you've any idea yourself?'

'No,' said Blaney. 'Sorry I can't help you there. It's always been a mystery where he came from in the first place, and where he hid out between jobs.'

Early the following morning, Blair left for a small town called Larimee, which the sheriff had told him was close to the Circle T Ranch. He arrived late in the afternoon, and dismounted outside the livery stable. The owner, Bert Brogan, who was standing in the stable entrance, greeted Blair.

'Howdy,' he said.

'Howdy,' said Blair. 'Can I leave my horse here for the night?'

'Sure,' said Brogan. 'I've got plenty of room. I'll feed and water him right away.'

'Maybe you can help me,' said Blair. 'I'm trying to catch up with a friend of mine. His folks told me he was riding this way.'

He gave Brogan a detailed description of Mulvaney. 'Happen you've seen him around?' he asked.

'I sure have,' said Brogan. 'About a month ago. He stabled his horse here. Only stayed two nights, and didn't talk a lot.'

'Sounds like him,' said Blair.

'Didn't seem like a fit man,' Brogan went on. 'I did hear that he rode out to the Circle T Ranch, three miles west of here, to see Hiram Trent.'

'Hiram Trent?' said Blair. 'I've heard that name before. How long has he been here?'

'About two years,' replied Brogan.

'Around five years ago,' said Blair, 'I met a Hiram Trent in Colorado. What does this Trent at the Circle T look like?'

'Tall and thin,' replied Brogan, 'with grey hair and a goatee beard. Always pretty smartly dressed.'

'That ain't anything like the Hiram Trent I knew,' said Blair. 'I guess they're two different people.'

'If you want to ask him about your friend,' said Brogan, 'he'll be in town tomorrow morning. He comes in once a week around ten to see the banker and one or two other people. Never misses. Usually rides back to the ranch around one.'

'Do any of his men come in with him?' asked Blair.

'No,' replied Brogan. 'He's always alone.'

'I'll see him tomorrow morning,' said Blair. 'Maybe he can tell me where my friend was heading when he left here.'

Blair stayed in the hotel overnight. He rose early and went for his horse. He told Brogan that he was intending to see Trent later on in the morning. He went in the store to make a few purchases, then rode out of town, towards the Circle T. About two miles out of town the trail ran close to a grove of cottonwood trees. Blair dismounted, led his horse well into the grove, and tied it to a tree. Taking his lariat and his field glasses with him, he walked back to the boundary of the grove, close to the trail.

Concealed inside the grove, Blair kept watch on the trail coming from the Circle T ranch house. At about fifteen minutes before ten he saw a rider approaching at a slow canter along the trail. Through the glasses, when the rider drew closer, Blair could see that he was the man Brogan had described to him the previous day.

Blair, holding the loop of his lariat in his right hand and the coils in his left, concealed himself in the grove as Trent cantered past. Then he quickly ran out behind the rancher, and chasing him silently from behind, he made an overheard toss for Trent's head. The loop fell down over the rancher's shoulders. Blair jerked it tight, and with a powerful heave he pulled Trent out of the saddle. The rancher fell heavily to the ground, his arms pinned to his sides.

Blair ran up to him, took his six-gun, and quickly trussed him so that he could not move. He went for the rancher's horse, which had stopped thirty yards along the trail, and led it to the centre of the grove, out of sight of any passing rider. Then he went back to Trent and dragged him to where his horse was standing. He looked down at the rancher.

Trent, enraged, was looking up at him. 'Whoever you are,' he said, his voice shaking with anger, 'you've made a bad mistake. Don't you know who I am?'

'I know exactly who you are, Trent,' said Blair. 'You're the rancher who was expecting to buy a stolen trail herd of 2,000 head from Mulvaney the outlaw.'

'I don't know what you're talking about,' said Trent.

'But Mulvaney never delivered that stolen herd, did he, Trent?' said Blair. 'It may interest you to know that when Mulvaney first stole that herd he murdered seven good men, all friends of mine.'

'I know nothing about that,' said Trent. He was beginning to look a worried man.

'I know,' Blair went on, 'that Mulvaney came here to see you about a month ago, to tell you that he had lost the herd. What I don't know, and what you're going to tell me, is just where Mulvaney was going when he left here.'

Trent licked his lips, 'I don't know,' he said. 'He never told me.'

Blair had a strong feeling that he was lying. 'Let's see if we can jog your memory,' he said.

He tied Trent's hands together in front of him, using a short length of rope from his own saddlebag. Then he unwound the lariat from Trent's body, leaving the noose around his neck. He ordered Trent, at gunpoint, to mount his horse. Then he threw the free end of the lariat over a branch of the cottonwood under which they were standing. Pulling on the free end, so that the noose tightened around Trent's neck, he secured it near the bottom of the tree.

From a bush close by he broke off a pliable piece of wood four feet long. Then he spoke to Trent. 'Unless you tell me what I want to know,' he said, 'I'm going to slap this horse hard on the flank. And if you do talk and I find out you've lied to me, I'm coming back here with the law. This is your last chance to stay alive.' As Blair raised his arm, Trent panicked.

'All right!' he shouted. 'All *right!* He has a cousin runs a small ranch somewhere east of Caldwell, Kansas. It's on the west bank of the Arkansas River. Mulvaney was going to rest up there a spell on account of a gunshot wound. And that's all I know.'

'What's the name of this cousin?' asked Blair.

'I don't know,' shouted Trent. 'Mulvaney never told me.'

Looking at Trent's face, Blair was pretty sure that he was telling the truth. He removed the lariat from the cottonwood and mounted his horse. He took the noose from Trent's neck, but left the rancher's hands tied.

'We're going for a ride,' he said. 'You in front. Try and escape and I'll shoot you down. We'll ride south until dark, then I'll turn you loose. Count yourself lucky I didn't hang you a few minutes ago.'

At nightfall, Blair released Trent, and watched the rancher as he rode off to the north. They had encountered no one during their ride together.

## TEN

The following day, Blair crossed the Kansas border and headed for Caldwell, a cattle town close to the border between Kansas and Indian Territory. When he eventually arrived there he located the county sheriff's office and went inside.

Tom Tyburn, the sheriff, was seated at his desk. He was a tall, lean man, with a luxuriant moustache which extended down both sides of his mouth. Blair had heard of his reputation as a respected law officer. He introduced himself and told Tyburn about the theft of his trail herd and his pursuit of Mulvaney. Tyburn listened with considerable interest.

'I just heard this morning,' he said, 'about Mulvaney losing all his men. You sure did a good job there. Mulvaney and his gang have been wanted men here for a long time.'

'I was told,' said Blair, 'that Mulvaney was going to stay for a while with a cousin of his who runs a small ranch somewhere east of here, by the Arkansas River. Do you know of any kin of his around here?'

'No, I don't,' replied Tyburn. 'And I ain't met the owners of the ranches out that way. There's been no reason for me to visit them since I took over here.'

'What I heard about Mulvaney coming here might not be true,' said Blair, 'but I think it is. He ordered the killing of seven of my men and I figure to ride east to the Arkansas River and see if I can find any trace of him.'

'If you do locate him,' said Tyburn, 'let me know and I'll get a posse out there pronto.'

'If he's there, and I get the chance, I'll be sure to let you know,' promised Blair.

He left Caldwell the following morning, riding east, and in the afternoon he rode into the small town of Meridew, not far from the Arkansas River. At the livery stable where he left his horse he asked the liveryman, Harper, how many ranches there were in the vicinity.

'Three,' replied Harper. 'All on the small side, close to the Arkansas.'

'I'm looking for work as a ranch hand,' said Blair. 'You reckon any of those ranches might take me on?'

'It ain't likely,' said the liveryman. 'As far as I know they've all got plenty of help. You could ask at two of them. They're both run by couples in their thirties, with young children. But I wouldn't advise going to the third one, that's the one right on the border with Indian Territory, about four miles east of here.'

'Why's that?' asked Blair.

'The owner, Bundy, is a surly man,' said Harper, 'and he's let it be known in town that visitors ain't welcome, and trespassers are liable to be shot. I heard he's put up a notice board on his property saying just that.

'He has a couple of hands working for

him,' Harper went on, 'and there's talk of a half-breed Indian woman living with him, but nobody's ever seen her around here. He has visitors now and again, but we never see them in town either.'

'You've persuaded me,' said Blair, 'not to go to Bundy's place asking for work.'

Leaving his horse with Harper for feed and water, and telling him he would collect it later, Blair walked over to the hotel. This Bundy character, he thought, was definitely worth investigating. He might well be the cousin with whom Mulvaney was staying.

After taking a meal in the hotel dining-room, Blair collected his horse from the livery stable and rode east out of town, as darkness was falling. About two miles out of Meridew the trail forked, the right fork carrying straight on, the left one angling to the north-east.

He chose the right fork, and two miles further on he rode into what appeared to be a narrow valley. He could see the dim outlines of high ground on either side, and the indistinct shapes of cattle lying on the ground nearby. He felt sure he must be on Bundy's ranch, but there was no sign yet of the ranch buildings.

He stayed on the trail, which ran along one side of the valley, and a short distance further on he stopped as he saw a stout post standing at the side of the trail with a large board fixed to the top. On the board, in letters painted so large that he could easily read them in the dim light, he saw the warning TRESPASSERS WILL BE SHOT. He was sure now that he was in the right spot.

He continued along the trail for another 200 yards, then stopped. To his left was the entrance to a large basin set in the slope bordering the valley, and in this sheltered basin he could see the vague outlines of several buildings. Light was showing through the windows of two of them.

Blair dismounted and tied his horse to a small bush a little way back along the trail. Then he headed for the basin in which he had seen the buildings. His hope was that he would be able to creep up and see the occupants through the windows which were showing chinks of light. If he could establish that Mulvaney was there, he would ride back to Caldwell and notify Sheriff Tyburn.

Cautiously, he walked towards the buildings along a narrow path between two lines of fencing, whose purpose he could not fathom. He was forty yards from the nearest building when suddenly, without warning, the ground gave way beneath him and he fell vertically downwards for about eleven feet. He landed on soft earth, with bent knees, and although he was badly shaken, no bones were broken. He stood up and looked around.

Above him he could see the night sky through the remains of the covering of brush and turf which had concealed the hole. Feeling around with his hands, and striking a few matches, he discovered that he was in a pit about four feet long and four feet wide. The sides of the pit had been shored up with smooth planks of timber, set deep in the ground and nailed firmly together at the bottom of the pit. They were also secured at the top. There was no purchase on the planks for his hands and feet, and during a further exhaustive examination of the pit he could see no possible way in which he could escape from it unaided.

He had heard no sounds from above since he fell into the pit and it seemed that Bundy and the others were unaware of his presence. He sat in a corner of the pit, with his back against the wall and waited for the dawn.

It was an hour after sun-up before he was discovered. He heard a faint shout above, followed by the sound of voices drawing nearer. Then he heard another voice shouting out: 'Get back, you fools. Anybody looking down in there is risking a bullet through the head. Go get a shotgun, Frank.' Blair recognized the voice as that of Mulvaney.

Shortly after, Mulvaney shouted down to Blair. 'Whoever you are down there,' he said, 'throw your gun out if you don't want a couple of loads of buckshot in you.'

Blair threw his Peacemaker out of the pit, and shortly after Mulvaney, holding the shotgun in his hand, cautiously peered down at Blair. His face showed shocked disbelief as he recognized the man in the pit. He spoke to Bundy, who was now by his side, looking down at the prisoner.

'We've got a big prize here, Frank,' he said. 'That was a good idea of yours to dig that pit to catch anybody snooping around here. The man down there is the one who killed off all the Mulvaney gang, except myself. I figure he's been looking for me because he wants to finish the job. Just how he managed to find me here, I don't know, but I aim to find out.

'It's clear he's on his own,' he went on. 'His horse will be around somewhere. Send one of the men to look for it, and bring a rope here.'

When Bundy returned with a rope, they dropped the end down to Blair. He tied it around his chest, under the arms, and the two men pulled him out of the pit. Mulvaney covered him with his six-gun, while Bundy searched him for further weapons and took his knife from him. Looking at Bundy, Blair could see that he was cast in the same mould as Mulvaney, a little stockier than his cousin, but with the same brutal and ruthless look about him.

'Well, well,' said Mulvaney, when Bundy had finished his search. 'I never figured, Calhoun, that we'd meet up again so soon. You've saved me the job of tracking you down and making you pay for what you did to my men. But before I do that, I've got to find out just how you found me here. Somebody must've done some talking. I've got to know who it was, so it don't happen again. We don't want nobody else snooping around here, do we Frank?'

'I can tell you who talked, Mulvaney,' said Blair. 'It was your old friend Hiram Trent of the Circle T. But he didn't have much choice. He was sitting on a horse at the time, with a noose around his neck fixed to a rope I'd slung over the branch of a cottonwood tree. He told me where to find you.'

Mulvaney turned as one of Bundy's men rode up, leading Blair's horse.

'He was on his own,' said the hand. 'There was no sign out there of anybody else riding with him.'

'Good,' said Mulvaney, then turned back to Blair.

'I believe what you say about Hiram Trent,' he said, 'but Trent didn't know exactly where I was. I'm curious to find out how you hit on this place. If you could do it, perhaps somebody else can. I want to have a talk with you about this before I finish you off for good.

'But that's going to have to wait till tomorrow,' he went on, 'because I've got some urgent business to attend to right now.'

He turned to Bundy. 'I'll be back before midnight, Frank,' he said. 'Keep Calhoun in the house, in the storeroom. Tie him up, and don't give him any food or drink. Then, tomorrow, I'll have a chat with him. And remember, we don't want him to die too easy. While I'm away you can think up some ways of making him suffer for what he's done. I know you're good at that sort of thing.'

One of the hands moved a hinged portion of each fence so that the two ends of the pit were blocked off, to prevent anyone accidentally falling into it during the daytime. Watching them, Blair realized that the purpose of the two fences was to channel any intruder towards the pit during the night.

Looking up the basin towards the slope leading to the high ground bordering the valley, Blair could see a stretch of what looked like soft, bare ground, and on one side of the basin a circular patch of thick brush about ten yards in diameter.

As soon as the pit had been blocked off, Bundy and the hand took Blair into the house. As they entered the living-room Blair saw a girl sweeping the floor. He guessed she was a half-caste Indian, in her late teens. She was an attractive-looking girl, with delicate features, and graceful in her movements. Her beauty was marred somewhat by two ugly bruises, one on each side of her face.

She looked up as Blair was brought in, and as she stared at him for a long moment, he could see the look of misery and despair on her face. Then she averted her head and continued sweeping.

They took Blair into the storeroom, a small room off the living-room. There they bound him hand and foot and left him sitting on the floor, his back to the wall. As Bundy closed the storeroom door behind him, he secured it with a heavy bolt.

Blair looked around. The walls of the room were lined with shelves carrying an assortment of articles. In one wall was a small open window about twelve inches square. Through it, he could hear Mulvaney and Bundy talking outside the house, then the sound of a horse and rider moving off.

He looked around again. He could see no way of escape. He was too well bound to free himself, and even if he had been able to do this, the window was too small to pass through and the door was well bolted on the outside. He stayed where he was, sitting on the floor, and forced himself to relax.

A couple of hours after he had been put in the room, Blair heard someone shouting on the other side of the door. It sounded like Bundy. Then he heard a woman cry out several times. After that there was silence until darkness was falling, when he heard the sound of the voices of Mulvaney and Bundy in the living-room. Mulvaney was telling Bundy that he had brought a supply of liquor back from town and he suggested that they and the two hands should have a game of poker after supper.

Soon after this the door opened and

Mulvaney walked into the room, holding his six-gun. He holstered it when he saw that Blair was sitting, still bound, on the floor.

'I just looked in, Calhoun,' he said, 'to let you know what I've been doing today. I've been sending a message to three old friends of mine to tell them I'm figuring on joining up with them soon. It won't be long before the Mulvaney gang is riding again.'

'Do they know just how you lost all your gang, Mulvaney?' asked Blair. 'If they do, maybe they won't be so keen on joining up with a leader who can't look after his men.'

Mulvaney flushed with anger. 'I'll see you in the morning, Calhoun,' he said, hoarsely. Then he turned abruptly and left the room.

Later in the evening Blair heard the hands come in for the poker game, and as the night wore on, it was clear from the noise they were making that the liquor was flowing freely. When the game finally broke up and the two hands left, Blair guessed that it was well after midnight. He heard Bundy and Mulvaney talking as they climbed the stairs to their bedrooms. Then silence descended on the house.

Blair dozed for a while, but was jerked into wakefulness when the room door was opened, and quickly closed again. A match was struck, and by its light he could see the girl staring down at him. He noticed a bruise on her jaw which had not been there when he saw her last. She touched her finger to her lips, then lit an oil lamp standing on one of the shelves. Blair sensed that she was trembling with fear. She bent down and whispered to him.

'I have heard them talking of you,' she said. 'I know you are a good man. If I cut these ropes, will you take me with you?'

As Blair nodded, she took a sharp kitchen knife from the large bag she had brought into the room, and sliced through the ropes around his wrists and ankles. He stood up and flexed his arms and legs. She picked the bag up, took a six-gun from it, and handed the weapon to Blair. Checking it, he found that the hammer was broken, so the gun could not be fired.

'Are Bundy and Mulvaney both in their rooms?' he asked her.

'Yes,' she whispered. 'They are both upstairs.'

'Follow me then,' said Blair, turning the lamp down a little, and handing it to her. He was still holding the six-gun in his hand. Slowly, he opened the door and walked into the living-room, the girl following closely behind him. He was heading for the door leading outside, when his eye caught a movement near the foot of the stairs. A man was descending them, swaying a little and grasping the handrail.

Blair ran up to the man as he reached the last tread and struck him hard across the head with the barrel of his revolver. The man's shout of warning was cut short as he collapsed. Blair caught hold of him and eased him on to the floor at the foot of the stairs, where he lay, motionless. Blair could see now that it was Bundy.

He listened for a moment. There was no

sound from upstairs, but whether Mulvaney had been alerted or not, he did not know. There was no time to lose. Looking at the clock standing on the sideboard, he could see that it was about one hour before dawn.

'In the bag,' whispered the girl, 'there is food and water, and also the money they took from you.'

He took the bag from her and they left the house. She followed Blair as he ran towards the back of the basin, along the stretch of soft, bare ground which Blair had noticed the previous day. When it petered out, to be replaced by hard ground leading up the slope, Blair carried on another twenty yards, then stopped. From the bag he took a small loaf of bread and dropped it on the ground, assuming that Mulvaney would think they had dropped it accidentally, in their haste to escape.

Then, keeping close together, they circled back, treading lightly and avoiding the soft ground, and took refuge in the patch of brush which Blair had seen earlier. Sitting down inside it, they were concealed from anyone passing by.

After a while they heard the sound of shouting from below. Blair peered out of the brush, and the light was now good enough for him to see Mulvaney and Bundy at the door of the shack in which the two hands slept. Bundy was holding his hand to his head. The two hands came out of the shack and the four men ran to the pasture and saddled the five horses there.

They mounted, one of them holding the reins of Blair's horse. Mulvaney and one of the hands started riding up the basin, while Bundy and the other hand rode out of the basin towards the trail running along the valley. When Mulvaney reached the tracks left in the soft ground by Blair and the girl, he stopped, examined them for a moment, then pulled his gun and fired a single shot.

He waited for Bundy and the other hand to ride up to him, then all four riders followed the tracks until they petered out. Mulvaney rode up to the loaf of bread lying on the ground, got down to examine it, then remounted. The other three followed him as he headed for the top of the slope, vainly searching the hard ground for more tracks as he rode along.

Blair watched the men as they rode up to the high ground bordering the valley. When they reached the top of the slope, they halted for a while, looking in all directions. Then they divided, the four men riding off in different directions, presumably in the hope that this would bring a speedy end to their search for the fugitives.

As the four riders disappeared from view, Blair turned to the girl. She was sitting on the ground, staring at him, the fear of being caught showing on her face.

'It's all right,' said Blair. 'They've ridden out of the valley. But we must stay here today. If we leave, one of them will see us, for sure. There's no horse here for us to take. What is your name?'

'It is Anona,' said the girl.

As Blair patiently questioned her, the

story came out. Her father, Gregory Miller, was an Englishman, her mother a Cherokee woman. Her mother had died six months ago and she had continued living with her father in a house he had built in Indian Territory not far from a town called Dando. She thought it was about twenty miles south of the Kansas border. Her father worked there, in a livery stable.

Soon after her mother died, Anona told Blair, she had been at the house alone one day, when Bundy and his two men had called, asking for directions. Seeing that she was alone, they had started to search the house for money. While they were doing this Anona had picked up a shotgun standing in the corner of the room, and Bundy had narrowly escaped being blown apart before he forced the muzzle of the gun upwards. As it was, he got several pieces of buckshot in the side of his face and neck.

Incensed, Bundy had decided to take Anona with him. He needed someone to do the cooking and other household chores back at the ranch. He had forced her to go along with them, riding a horse taken from the pasture. When they reached the ranch in Kansas, she found that she was a virtual prisoner, locked in her bedroom at night and doing the housework during the daytime. If she displeased Bundy in any way, she was rewarded by a beating.

Anona went on to tell Blair that she had twice tried to escape, but each time had been caught and severely beaten. She had hoped at first that her father might find her, but as time went on, that hope had faded away. Then, the previous night, she had heard Bundy, after a spell of heavy drinking, stumble his way up the stairs and go into his room.

His customary practice, as he passed her door, was to turn the key in the lock, but on this occasion, his mind obviously befuddled by liquor, he omitted to do this; so she was able, when Mulvaney and Bundy were sleeping, to free Blair.

'It is over now, Anona,' said Blair, smiling

at her. 'Soon, I will take you back to your father. Tonight, after it is dark, we will leave here.'

She looked at him, scarcely daring to hope that her long ordeal was over.

Not expecting that Mulvaney or any of the others would be returning for a while, Blair, careful to leave no tracks, ran to the house then to the shack being used by the two hands, and searched them for weapons. But he found none. He returned to the girl and they ate some of the food which she had placed in the bag.

The men who had been searching for them returned a little before dark. Mulvaney was the first to appear. They saw him put his horse in the pasture, then walk up to the tracks left by Blair and Anona in the soft ground. As he was following the tracks up the slope, Bundy and his two men arrived below.

Mulvaney stopped where the tracks faded away. He looked at the bread still lying on the ground ahead, then back towards the buildings. Then he circled back, as the two fugitives had done, and approached the patch of brush in which they were hiding.

'Lie down,' whispered Blair, urgently, and they both prostrated themselves on the ground in the small open space they had cleared earlier.

Mulvaney stopped on the edge of the patch of brush, stood on tiptoe, and looked across the top of it. Then he took a step into the brush. As he did so, there came a shout from Bundy down below. Mulvaney halted, then turned and walked down to join the others.

When he reached them they all reported having seen no sign of the fugitives, although they had searched all the surrounding area in the vicinity of the ranch, and Bundy had checked that they had not been seen in Meridew.

'I can't figure it out,' said Mulvaney. 'Two people afoot, with not much of a start on us, and they vanish without a trace. I'm wondering if somehow they made it to that rough ground near the river. There's plenty of hiding places there. We'll have a look there at first light. And we'd better have two men waiting just outside Meridew all night, in case they turn up there. That's the place they'll most likely make for when they get the chance.'

Bundy spoke to his two hands, who, after a hurried meal, mounted their horses and rode towards town.

# ELEVEN

Blair and Anona waited until an hour after the lights in the house had gone out. Then they moved cautiously down to the pasture, which was a little way from the dwellings. There were three horses inside. After a short search, Blair located his own and led it to the gate. Then, fumbling in the darkness, he put on the horse a saddle and a bridle which were lying on the ground close to the gate. He mounted and helped Anona up behind him.

They left the valley by riding up the side of the shallow basin, then headed west, bypassing the town of Meridew. They reached Caldwell just as dawn was breaking. Blair asked a man on the street where Sheriff Tyburn lived, and they rode along to a neat, white-fenced house on the edge of town.

After a short interval, Tyburn answered the knock on the door. His eyes widened at the sight of Blair and the girl. He stood back and beckoned them inside, at the same time calling to his wife. She came in a moment later. Shocked at the sight of the bruises on the girl's face, she took Anona's arm and sat her down in the living-room. The two men followed behind.

Blair told the Tyburns of the events which had taken place since he was last in Caldwell, and of the kidnapping of Anona by Bundy.

'If we ride now,' he told Tyburn, 'there's just a slim chance that we might catch Mulvaney and the others.'

Tyburn rose quickly from his chair. 'I'm going for two of my deputies,' he said, 'and I'll call in a couple of townspeople. With you along as well, that'll make a posse of six. You wait here. I'll be back for you in half an hour.'

When the sheriff had left, Blair turned to Mrs Tyburn.

'While I'm away,' he said, 'I want Anona to be in a safe place. Can you think of somewhere I can leave her where she'll be treated right? When I come back I'm going to take her to her father in Indian Territory.'

'She stays right here,' said Mrs Tyburn, a plump, grey-haired, motherly woman. 'I hope you catch that villain Bundy. Stealing a girl from her father like that don't bear thinking about. First thing I'm going to do is bathe those bruises and put some ointment on. Then we can think about finding some nice clothes for Anona. She wants to look good when she meets her pa.' Putting her arm around Anona's shoulders, she led her from the room.

The posse rode to the Bundy ranch as fast as they could, but when they arrived there, all four men had gone, and there were no signs of them in the vicinity.

'I guess they took fright when they found my horse was missing,' said Blair.

Until night came, they searched the area outside the valley for the tracks of the four men's horses, without success. Then they rode back to Caldwell. The sheriff took Blair to his house and Mrs Tyburn invited him to have supper with them.

Anona was already looking a lot better. The sheriff's wife had found her a colourful dress from somewhere, and had helped her fix her hair. After supper, she went to bed and Blair had a talk with the sheriff.

'We'll carry on looking for Mulvaney and the others tomorrow,' said Tyburn. 'But I ain't got much hope of finding them. I reckon they're clear out of the county by now.'

'I'll take Anona to her father tomorrow,' said Blair. 'Then I'll come back here. If you don't find those four tomorrow, I've got an idea how we might find out just where Mulvaney's going.'

He told Tyburn about Mulvaney saying that he'd sent a message to three friends of his, telling them that he would be joining up with them with the idea of forming a new Mulvaney gang.

175

'I'm pretty sure,' said Blair, 'that he sent that message from the telegraph office in Meridew exactly two days ago. If you could see copies of those messages, or if the telegraph operator could remember what they were, they would probably say just where the men were to meet Mulvaney. If I knew that, I could go there and get in touch with the local lawman, if there's one in the area.'

'That's a good idea,' said the sheriff. 'While you're away I'll check with the telegraph operator at Meridew.'

Blair spent the night at the hotel and in the morning he went to the store and bought some supplies, and pants, vest and shirt for Anona. Then he went to the livery stable to hire a horse for the girl. When he arrived at the sheriff's house, Anona changed, and they were ready to leave. He could see that she was getting excited at the prospect of reuniting with her father.

They took their leave of the sheriff and his wife and soon crossed the border into

Indian Territory. Blair had taken directions from the sheriff and they rode into Dando in the early afternoon. Blair followed Anona as she headed for the livery stable along the street on the left.

A tall man was sweeping the ground just outside the stable door. He glanced casually at the two approaching riders, then resumed sweeping, but suddenly stopped abruptly and looked at them again.

'Father!' shouted Anona, jumping down from her horse and running up to him. Hardly able to believe what he was seeing, Miller took her into his arms and held her tightly as she dissolved into tears. A few passers-by collected to observe the scene and the livery stable owner came out of the stable to see what was happening.

'This is a great day for you, Greg,' he said, when Anona had quietened a little. 'I sure am glad to see your girl back again. You just stop what you're doing and take her home. I don't want to see you back here today, and take a few more days off if you want.'

Blair rode with Anona and her father to their house. It was a small, well-built timber structure, a little east of town. Inside the house they sat down while Anona told her father of her experiences since he had last seen her. Blair filled in for her here and there. When she had finished, Miller turned to Blair.

'I sure am beholden to you, Mr Calhoun,' he said, 'for getting Anona back to me. I just couldn't figure out where she'd gone, or who'd taken her. I searched for a long time, but couldn't find any trace of her. In the end, I had to give up.'

A little later, Anona left them to prepare a meal, and Miller told Blair a little of his past.

'I came out from England as a single man,' he said, 'and started working my way west. While I was heading for Dando I came across a young Cherokee woman. She was lying in a ravine about four miles east of here, badly beaten and near starving to death. She'd been thrown out of her village because of false stories some of the other women had spread about her.

'She was a beautiful woman,' he said, 'just like Anona is now. I took care of her; built a shelter for us first, then this house. When she died, if it hadn't been for Anona, I reckon I'd have gone to pieces.'

Blair accepted Miller's invitation to stay the night, and left for Caldwell the following morning, taking back with him the horse he had hired for Anona. Arriving at Caldwell, he returned the horse to the livery stable, then rode on to the sheriff's office, dismounted, and went inside. Tyburn was at his desk.

The sheriff told Blair that they had found no sign of Mulvaney and the others the previous day, but that he had called at the telegraph office in Meridew and the operator remembered a stranger fitting the description of Mulvaney who had sent a telegraph message on the day concerned. The operator had had a busy day and he didn't recall the contents of the message, but he was absolutely sure that it had been sent to a man called Parker in the Denver area. The reason he remembered this was because his own name was Parker.

'I reckon,' said Blair, 'that Mulvaney may have picked up a Kansas Pacific Railroad train at Ellsworth to get him to Denver. I'm going to ride up to Ellsworth and go by train myself. It'll be a lot quicker that way.'

'A good idea,' said Tyburn. 'If I get any more information about Mulvaney that I figure you'd like to have, I'll send it on to Sheriff Riley in Denver for you. He's a good man. I knew him when we were deputies together in Abilene. Be sure to give him my regards.'

Two days later, Blair boarded the Denver train at Ellsworth. Enquiries of the station staff revealed that a man answering Mulvaney's description had boarded the Denver train two days before. He had been alone. As Blair sat in the train, watching the prairie slip by, he wondered where Bundy and his two hands had gone.

On arrival at Denver Blair checked with the station whether anybody remembered Mulvaney's arrival. But he drew a blank. He walked to the sheriff's office and found Sheriff Riley inside. He introduced himself, briefly explained the reason for his presence in Denver, and passed on Sheriff Tyburn's greetings.

Riley asked a few questions about his old friend, then he studied Blair with interest.

'There's a whole heap of law officers and honest citizens,' he said, 'who raised a loud cheer when word got around of what you did to the Mulvaney gang. And as for Mulvaney himself, I'm just as keen to get my hands on him as you are.'

'This man Parker,' said Blair. 'The man Mulvaney sent a message to. Does the name mean anything to you?'

'It's a common name, of course,' said Riley, 'but the man could be an outlaw of that name we've been after for some time. He works with two other men, McKay and Webster, on bank and stagecoach robberies.

They don't seem too well organized; in fact they've made a mess of some of their operations. But they've never been caught. It looks as if they may be hiding out somewhere in this area. And if Mulvaney takes charge, they're going to be a lot more of a problem than they have been up to now.'

'D'you think we'll get any useful information at the telegraph office here?' asked Blair.

'We'll soon find out,' said Riley. 'Let's go over there.'

The operator remembered the message for Parker, but not the contents. It had been collected at the telegraph office by a man called Parker who called in occasionally to see if there were any messages for him. The operator had no idea where Parker was living, but he was pretty sure it was somewhere out of town; and probably not all that far, because he had always turned up at the telegraph office before noon. His description of Parker seemed to match the sketchy details of the outlaw's appearance in the sheriff's files.

Blair and Riley returned to the sheriff's office, after Riley had asked the operator to let him know immediately if Parker turned up again.

'Looks like Parker and the other two are hiding out somewhere not far from here,' said Riley. 'I'd give a lot to know just where they are.'

'You and your men can watch out for them in town, of course,' said Blair, 'but I don't think it's likely Mulvaney will show his face in Denver. I'm sure he knows that I'm still on his trail. Have you got a description of the other two men, McKay and Webster, who work with Parker?'

'No,' replied the sheriff. 'All I have is that rough description of Parker himself.'

'What I'll do,' said Blair, 'is have a ride around the area, within a radius of twenty miles or so from Denver, and see if I can spot any sign of their hideout.'

'Right,' said Riley. 'And if you see anything

183

suspicious while you're looking around, get in touch with me right away.'

'I'll do that,' promised Blair.

Denver, the 'mile-high city', bounded on one side by the Rocky Mountain range, was founded when gold was discovered in 1858 along the South Platte River. Other gold finds followed in the area, but by the late 1860s the gold bonanza had petered out. But once again prospectors flooded into the area when high-grade silver ore was discovered in large quantities in 1869. In his search of the area, Blair was to see many signs of past and present mining activities.

He carried out his search systematically, by dividing the area of search into sectors, each of a size which could, he estimated, be covered in one day's ride out of Denver and back. He started the operation on the west side of town.

On the first day of his search he found no trace of Mulvaney and the others. On the second day, in the foothills of the Rockies, in a narrow ravine, he came across an old prospector sitting on the ground holding his bandanna against a wound on the side of his head. A mule and a burro were standing nearby. The burro's load was scattered on the ground.

The wounded man tried to rise as he saw Blair approaching, but his legs buckled beneath him and he fell flat on his back on the ground. Blair dismounted, and helped him to sit up.

'My name's Calhoun,' he said. 'Looks like you're in trouble. Let me look at that wound.'

'I'm obliged,' said the prospector. 'My name's Tasker, Will Tasker.'

He remained quiet while Blair thoroughly washed the wound with water from the trickle running down the ravine.

'You got any bandages?' asked Blair.

Tasker pointed to a saddlebag on the mule. Blair took a length of bandage out, made a pad with a piece of it, then secured the pad in position with a length of bandage wound tightly around the head.

'I reckon that'll do for the time being,' said

Blair. 'I'm making a guess you were pistol-whipped.'

'You're darned right I was,' said Tasker, indignantly. 'Four armed robbers rode up and one of them bent a gun over my head. Then they went through my things till they found my bag of gold-dust. That was all I had to show for all those years of prospecting. I reckon the dust in there was worth a couple of thousand dollars at today's prices.'

Blair pricked up his ears at the mention of the four robbers. Was it possible, he wondered, that Mulvaney, with Parker and the others, had decided that robbing the mining fraternity was more profitable than rustling cattle or stealing from banks and stagecoaches? He asked Tasker to describe the four men.

The builds of two of the men the prospector described were similar to the builds of Mulvaney and Parker, but nothing Tasker could tell Blair was sufficient to identify them as such without any doubt.

'As it happens,' said Tasker, 'I'm pretty sure I know where them four robbers are hanging out.'

'You are?' asked Blair, surprised.

Tasker explained that two days ago, early in the morning, he had been prospecting some high ground about three miles south of his present position, when he had spotted what looked like an abandoned shack in the valley below. Four horses, three chestnuts and a pinto, were grazing near the shack. Curious, he had watched the shack from cover, and after a short time four men had come out, similar in build to the four men who had recently attacked him. They mounted the horses and rode off.

'I'm sure they were the ones who robbed me,' said Tasker. 'I recognized both the men and the horses.'

'How're you feeling?' asked Blair. 'Would you like me to take you to see a doctor in Denver?'

'There ain't no need for that,' said Tasker, getting to his feet. 'I'm all right now. Was just a little shaky for a while there.'

'If you think you're up to it,' said Blair, 'would you take me to that shack you've just been talking about? Maybe we can get your gold-dust back.'

Tasker looked doubtful. 'You sure?' he asked. 'I ain't much of a fighting man at my age, and there's four of them. And a mean-looking bunch, at that.'

'My idea was to try and get the dust back without tangling with the robbers,' said Blair.

'I'm with you, then,' said Tasker, and with Blair's help he loaded up the burro.

They travelled slowly, and Tasker took a circuitous route to bring them to the point from which he had previously looked down on the shack in the valley. The same four horses were visible grazing near the shack. As Blair and his companion watched, four men came out of the shack and stood, apparently talking to each other.

Blair took his field glasses from his saddlebag and studied each of the four men in turn. He quickly realized, with considerable disappointment, that neither Mulvaney nor Parker was in the group. He turned to Tasker as the four men walked back into the shack.

'We'll stay here for the night,' he said. 'I have a feeling those robbers'll be riding off in the morning to do some more thieving. Then we can have a look inside the shack.'

Blair's surmise turned out to be correct. Shortly after daybreak, as he and Tasker were watching the shack, the four men came out, saddled their horses, and rode off to the west. Half an hour later, Blair and his companion rode down to the shack. While Tasker kept watch outside the door Blair went inside and looked around.

He thought that there was a good chance that the proceeds of recent robberies were hidden there, because there would be disadvantages in carrying them around all the time. But if they were in the shack, they would be well-hidden from any casual passer-by.

There was no furniture, apart from a table, on which some provisions were standing, and four rickety chairs. Bedrolls and blankets were piled up in a corner. There were no hiding-places on the walls or in the roof, and there were no signs that the dirt floor had recently been disturbed. Then Blair's eye fell on the big iron stove. He walked up to it and examined it closely.

The stove was standing on a flat piece of timber. The chimney pipe passed loosely through a hole in the roof. He lifted the pipe off and tried to move the heavy stove sideways, but had to call Tasker in to help him. They slid it off the wooden base, then Blair lifted the piece of timber to reveal a circular hole in the ground containing a large number of bank-notes and several bags of gold-dust. Tasker immediately identified his own bag on top of the pile. Quickly, they lifted out the whole of the contents of the hole, placed them in a strong empty sack which they found lying in a corner, and loaded this on to the burro.

They replaced the wooden base over the hole, slid the stove on to it, and replaced the chimney pipe. Then, leaving no signs of their presence inside the shack, they left the valley, heading for Denver. As they rode along, Blair told the prospector of the reason for his presence in the area and of his search for Mulvaney and the others.

Tasker thought hard for a short while when Blair had finished. Then he spoke.

'Maybe I can help,' he said. 'I've been prospecting in this area for quite a while now. I know most of what's going on around here, and I've met a lot of the miners.

'There was something I saw that struck me as a bit odd,' he went on. 'About three weeks ago I was well up in the foothills west of Denver where there are some abandoned mines. I was sitting down having a rest when I spotted three horsemen riding up to the boarded-up entrance to an abandoned mine tunnel dug into the hillside.

'I kept well down out of sight,' he continued, 'and watched them take the boarding down and all go into the tunnel, taking their horses with them. Then they put the boarding back again behind them. I was there about an hour, and they were still inside when I left. I can't deny that I was mighty curious about what they were doing in there, but I wasn't fool enough to try and find out and get myself shot.

'But you said it was four men you were after,' Tasker went on, 'so likely these weren't the ones.'

'They could be,' said Blair, 'because at the time you're speaking of, Mulvaney hadn't joined up with Parker and the others. Can you tell me just where that tunnel is?'

When Blair had obtained the exact location of the abandoned mine from Tasker he told the prospector that he was going to ride ahead and suggest to Sheriff Riley that he take a posse out without delay to arrest the men who had robbed him of his gold-dust. Leaving Tasker to follow, he rode on fast to the sheriff's office in Denver. Riley was just leaving the office as he arrived. He turned and went back inside with Blair.

Blair told him of the attack on Tasker and of the recovery of the gang's loot. He told the sheriff that if he got a posse organized quickly there was a good chance of catching the four robbers.

'This *is* good news,' said Riley. 'I've been looking for that gang for a while. I'll have a posse ready in twenty minutes. Can you come along to show us the way?'

'Sure,' agreed Blair. 'I'll be back here in twenty minutes.'

When the posse had assembled, Blair led it to the place from which he and Tasker had looked down on the shack. It was mid-afternoon. There was no sign of the men or their horses.

'I figure they'll most likely be turning up before dark,' said Blair.

'We'll wait here,' said Riley, 'till they've all gone into the shack. Then we'll go down the slope at the back of the shack. I don't see no window there. With a bit of luck we'll surprise them, and maybe we'll get away without any shooting.'

It was just over an hour later when the four robbers appeared in view. They rode up the valley, dismounted, and took the saddles off their horses. Then they all went inside the shack.

Fifteen minutes later, the posse, waiting at the top of the slope right behind the building, started moving down towards it as noiselessly as possible. They all reached the rear of the shack without being spotted, then moved around the side, ducking underneath the window as they passed. The door of the building was ajar.

They paused for a moment, then Riley pushed hard on the door and he and Blair stepped smartly into the shack. Riley was carrying a Remington 10-gauge shotgun with double barrels, aimed directly at the four men seated at the table. Startled, they looked at the intruders, and any thoughts of resistance they might have had were immediately abandoned at the sight of the lethal weapon in the sheriff's hands.

The deputies disarmed the four robbers, and they were taken back to Denver to await trial. Tasker came into the sheriff's office shortly after the posse's return and handed over to Riley the stolen gold-dust and bank-notes recovered from the shack earlier.

'A good day's work, and all thanks to you two,' said Riley, to Blair and the prospector. 'The miners around here have a lot to thank you for.'

A little later, Blair told the sheriff about Tasker's sighting, three weeks earlier, of three men entering the tunnel of an abandoned mine.

'There's just a chance it was Parker's hide-out,' he said, 'and if it was, Mulvaney could be there with them now. I'm going to ride up there overnight and watch that tunnel entrance through my field glasses tomorrow. If I find out that Mulvaney and the others are there, I'll come back here for help.'

Blair then confirmed the exact location of the tunnel with Tasker.

'You want me to come along?' the old man

asked him. 'I'm getting a taste for the sort of action we've been having lately.'

Smiling, Blair declined his offer. 'Better if this is a one-man operation,' he said.

# TWELVE

Blair had a few hours' sleep, then he headed for the mine. He arrived, just before dawn at a vantage point above it, from which, concealed, he could keep a close watch on the tunnel entrance. He could see that the boarding was in place over it.

For the next four hours he saw no signs of movement near the tunnel entrance. He thought it likely that, were the mine occupied, somebody would have come out before now. He went for his horse, mounted it, and rode down to the mine entrance. Reaching it, he stood against the heavy piece of boarding, noticing that it was not fixed into position, but was resting against the sides of the entrance. He pulled it towards him a little and listened through the gap. He could hear no sounds from inside.

He took a good look at the surrounding area through his field glasses. There was no one in sight. He moved the boarding to one side, then, leaving his horse outside, he walked into the tunnel for a few paces, then stood for a short while, to accustom his eyes to the darkness ahead. Then he walked for a short distance into the tunnel, illuminated dimly by the light coming in from outside.

About fifteen yards back from the entrance the tunnel suddenly widened, to form a circular space about twelve feet in diameter, then narrowed to its original width. Lighting an oil lamp which he found standing on the ground, Blair saw evidence that horses had been standing in the tunnel, and that people were occupying the circular area, but there was no indication as to their identity.

Still holding the lamp, Blair walked further along the tunnel. He could see that it had been abandoned for some time. The timber posts supporting the roof were in poor condition and the floor was scattered with debris from minor falls. After he had progressed about thirty yards without encountering an end to the tunnel, he retraced his steps.

When he reached the circular area he extinguished the lamp and left it where he had found it. He walked towards the entrance, but before he reached it he caught sight of four men outside, about thirty yards away, sprinting towards him with guns drawn. Immediately he recognized Mulvaney as one of the four. The sight of Blair's horse and the open entrance to the tunnel had obviously alerted them to danger.

Blair knew that if he ran out of the tunnel, he faced almost certain death at the hands of the four gunmen. Quickly he turned and ran back, through the wider section, and into the darkness further on. He was sure that Mulvaney would not have seen him clearly enough to recognize him.

In his haste he cannoned into one of the timber posts supporting the roof and felt it give way slightly under the impact. He had continued for a few more steps when, from behind him, he heard the ominous rumble of a large mass of falling debris. A moment later there was a smaller fall from directly above him, and he found himself partially buried, with only his head protruding from the pile. He was in complete darkness.

There was silence now, except for the patter of a few small pieces of rock as they fell from above. A dense cloud of dust in the air set Blair coughing. When it had settled, he began to clear away the rubble which was covering most of his body. When he had done this, he found that no bones had been broken, but he had numerous bruises and he felt a trickle of blood on his forehead where he had been struck by a large piece of rock.

He rested for a while in the darkness, reviewing the situation. From the sound of the fall, he guessed that a considerable section of the roof had collapsed between him and the tunnel entrance. It would, he thought, be an impossible task for him to try and tunnel through it without being trapped and killed by further falls. And what if he did achieve the impossible and work his way through? Would Mulvaney and the others be waiting on the other side to shoot him down?

Blair knew that sometimes miners dug intersecting tunnels. Maybe there was another exit from the mine. He decided to investigate. He had a few matches in his pocket, which would provide a little light when he really needed it.

He started walking along the tunnel, away from the fall, feeling his way past the supports with his hands, and checking the side walls for gaps. He made slow progress in the dark. Eventually, he came to what appeared to be the end of the tunnel. Striking a match to confirm this, he found himself facing a blank wall.

He stood for a moment. It seemed that he was trapped, with no hope of escape; and without food and water death would be inevitable. He turned, and slowly made his way back along the tunnel. Once again, he checked the side walls with his hands as he progressed.

He judged that he was about half-way back to the point where the roof had caved in, when he suddenly halted as he sensed the faintest hint of a current of air wafting on to his right cheek. He stood close to the right wall of the tunnel, and moved his head back and forth until he felt the air current quite distinctly. He felt the wall with his hand and found that there was an irregular vertical gap in it, varying between five to eight inches wide, which he had missed on his previous check.

He put his hand and arm through the gap, but could feel nothing on the other side. He struck a match and passed it through the gap. The flame flickered in the draught, but before it went out he saw what looked like another tunnel on the other side of the wall, a little narrower than the one he was standing in. The thickness of the rock wall between the two tunnels appeared to be around eight inches.

Why the tunnels had not been opened up to one another, Blair could only conjecture. Perhaps a sudden decision had been taken to stop working the mine when it became uneconomic to do so. In order to get through into the second tunnel he would have to find some way of widening the gap at one point into a circular hole big enough for his body to pass through. He walked back to the roof fall, counting his steps as he went along. When he reached it, he lit some matches and selected some pieces of the hardest rock, with sharp edges, that he could find. With these, he would try to enlarge the gap between the tunnels.

Taking the same number of steps back along the tunnel, he found the gap in the wall again, and working in the dark he started chipping the wall away to enlarge the gap at a point around four feet from the floor of the tunnel. With a heavy hammer and a steel chisel to work with, the job would have been easy, but he knew that, working in the dark, his only tool a piece of rock, he faced a formidable task, even through the wall material was, fortunately, somewhat softer than the pieces of rock he was using to enlarge the gap.

He started work as best he could in the dark, feeling for the gap with one hand, then striking out with the rock held in the other. He continued his efforts, with no idea of the passage of time. He rested from time to time, then restarted with renewed vigour. But gradually his strength flagged, the muscles in his right arm protested more and more, and progress grew slower.

But finally, just as he was approaching the limit of his endurance, he ran his hand around the hole and judged that it was large enough to take his body. In his exhausted state he had some difficulty in manoeuvring himself through to the other tunnel. When he had finally managed to do this, he sat on the floor for a while to recover his strength. This tunnel, he thought, providing there were no roof falls, would almost certainly lead him to the open air.

He got up and slowly made his way along the tunnel, feeling the slight current of air on his face. Eventually, he saw, ahead of him, a few small chinks of daylight and shortly after this he forced his way through a dense tangle of brush and stood in the open air. Looking at the sun, he realized that it was over twenty-four hours since he had been trapped by the fall. He stepped back into the cover of the brush, and looked around.

He could see, about forty yards away, the entrance to the tunnel which Mulvaney and the others had been using. The boarding was in place and there was no sign that anyone was around. He waited for an hour, watching the entrance and scanning the surrounding terrain to make sure no riders were near.

Then he ran across to the boarding, removed it, and entered the tunnel, gun in hand. He listened for a moment, but could hear no sounds. He walked along to the area where Mulvaney and the others had been sleeping. It was empty, and all traces of their having been there had been removed. It was clear that, alarmed by the presence of an intruder, even though they must have thought he was unlikely to stay alive, they had ridden off in search of a new hiding-place, taking Blair's horse with them.

He had a look for tracks in the vicinity, but was not able to decide in which direction the outlaws had ridden off when they abandoned the hide-out. He set off walking in the direction of Denver. The wound on his head was not serious, and had stopped bleeding some time ago. But his body ached from the pounding it had received when the roof fell in on him. He had covered about three miles, when he stopped at a stream, drank some water and washed the blood from his face.

He had just set off again, when he saw a sight which brought a smile of relief to his face. Rounding a small hill a quarter of a mile away, and coming towards him, was

Will Tasker, riding his mule and trailing his burro behind him. As the prospector came up to Blair, he looked at him in astonishment.

'What in tarnation happened to you?' he asked.

Blair explained.

'You heading for Denver?' asked Tasker.

'Yes,' said Blair. 'I've got to tell the sheriff about Mulvaney and the others.'

'Take the mule,' said Tasker, dismounting. 'I was figuring on staying here until noon tomorrow.'

'Thanks,' said Blair. 'I appreciate the loan. As soon as I reach Denver I'll have the mule brought back to you.'

'Better have something to eat before you leave,' said Tasker. 'I've got plenty here.'

Feeling better after taking some food, Blair continued on his way. When he reached Denver he called at the livery stable near the sheriff's office and the owner agreed to arrange for the mule to be returned to Tasker. Blair then walked along to see the sheriff.

Riley listened to his story with interest and concern. 'Seems like you're mighty lucky to be here,' he said. 'You got any idea where Mulvaney and the others have gone?'

'No,' replied Blair. 'They didn't leave any tracks I could follow. But I guess they've found another hiding-place by now. There must be dozens of places around here where they could hole up. What I'll do is to start riding round again like I did before, and go a bit further afield this time. I'll ask Tasker to keep his eyes open as well.'

'All right,' said Riley, 'but like I said before, let me know if you get any lead. Don't try tackling them on your own if you can help it.'

Blair spent the next two weeks looking for the outlaws' hide-out, without success. Returning to Denver on the last day of his search, he went to see Riley.

'Bad news,' said Riley, as Blair entered his office. 'The eastbound stage was held up two days ago, about ten miles out of

Denver, by four masked men. They killed the driver and blew the strongbox open. It was quite a haul for them, according to the stagecoach company.

'From the descriptions we got,' Riley went on, 'it could have been Mulvaney and the others. The leader was exactly the same size as Mulvaney, from what you've told me about him. I had a posse on the scene about four hours after the hold-up, but we didn't have any luck getting on their trail. Whoever they were, they made a very good job of hiding their tracks.'

'I've had no luck searching for their hide-out,' said Blair, 'and I've been thinking that a better idea might be to set a trap for them. But the plan I have in mind needs some co-operation from the editor of the *Denver News* and from the stagecoach company.'

'The editor, Nat Carling, is a friend of mine,' said Riley. 'I reckon he'll help if he can. The same goes for the stagecoach company. What d'you have in mind?'

'The thing that Mulvaney wants most is to

see me dead,' said Blair, 'and he don't take kindly to criticism and ridicule. What I figure on doing is to have a piece in the *News* that'll bring him and his gang out of hiding. I know the paper's pretty widely circulated and I figure that Mulvaney will be certain to get hold of a copy, if only to get news that might help him to plan his next robbery.'

'And the stagecoach?' asked Riley.

'I'm going to ride in the stagecoach from Denver to Pueblo,' said Blair. 'And I'm hoping I can fix it so that Mulvaney and the others hold up the coach with the idea of finishing me off. But I'd have to be the only passenger, and the driver would have to be somebody you'd deputized to go along. We can't risk innocent people being killed.

'What I had in mind,' Blair continued, 'was that you could take a posse quietly out of town, up into the foothills, before the coach left. Then, with a pair of field glasses, you could shadow the coach and when you spotted the Mulvaney gang making their play, you could ride down fast to help us out.'

'One thing I don't like about that plan,' said Riley, 'is that you and the driver'll be facing the gang alone till we can get to you.'

'I thought of having two of your deputies on the coach with me,' said Blair. 'Then I figured that one of Mulvaney's men – one of the two we don't have descriptions of – might be watching the stage leave, so he could ride hell-for-leather to Mulvaney, waiting along the route somewhere, to let him know whether or not I was on the stage. If he told Mulvaney there were two deputies with me, I'm pretty sure Mulvaney would call the operation off.'

'You're probably right,' said Riley, then thought hard for a few moments. 'I have an idea,' he said. 'The town marshal in Pueblo is my brother. I'm going to send him a letter on the next stage to ask if he can loan two deputies to ride with you. I'll ask him to have them dressed up as drummers, with no guns or badges showing, and to get them here before your stage leaves. And about the driver. I know just the man to drive that stagecoach to Pueblo. He lives here in Denver. He drove for a couple of years on the Overland Route. And he's pretty handy with a gun.'

'That's a good idea of yours,' said Blair, then spent some time discussing the operation in detail with Riley.

'I reckon it could work,' said the sheriff, when they had finished. 'I'm going to have words with Carling and the station manager for the stagecoach company right now to see how they feel about co-operating with us.'

'Right,' said Blair. 'While you're away I'll stay here and concoct the article for the *News*. If Carling agrees to help us, tell him I'll bring it along later.'

The sheriff left and Blair stayed on in the office, spending the next forty minutes working on a draft of what he hoped would form the basis of a news item in the *News*. He was just giving it a final going-over when Riley returned.

'Carling's willing to help,' said the sheriff, 'and Manley, the station manager, says there's no doubt that the stagecoach company headquarters will agree. He wants you to give him all the details of the plan just as soon as you can.'

'Good,' said Blair. 'I'll do that.' He handed his draft of the news item to Riley. 'This is what I'm taking to Carling,' he said. 'What d'you think?'

Riley read the draft twice, then turned to Blair.

'I can see this is going to rile Mulvaney considerably,' he said, 'which is just what you want.'

'That's right,' said Blair, 'and when a man's badly riled he don't often think as straight as he should.'

'I reckon this news item is just right,' said Riley, 'and I think there's a good chance of the plan working. But Carling'll probably want to fiddle around with the wording a bit. These editors seem to have a lingo of their own—a bit on the flowery side, I often

213

think. Seems to me they often use three or four words when one would be enough, and some of the words they use, half their readers don't understand the meaning of.'

'You're right,' agreed Blair, 'but I reckon we ain't got no choice but to let him have his head on this.'

Blair walked along to the newspaper office with his draft. He introduced himself to Carling, a tall, thin man wearing a natty bow tie, and handed the sheet over. Carling sat down at his desk and read the draft with interest.

'I understand what you're hoping this news item will achieve, Mr Calhoun,' he said. 'The necessary material's in there, but as it is now, it's a bit on the dull side. I'm going to ginger it up a little.'

He picked up a thick, black pencil, and muttering to himself as he went along, he made numerous additions, deletions and alterations to the text. When he had finished, he read it through, made a couple more changes, then handed it to Blair.

'There,' he said. 'That should do the trick.'
Blair looked at the text. It read:

## FAMOUS GANGBUSTER BLAIR CALHOUN VISITS DENVER

Denver is proud to welcome Blair Calhoun, who, single-handed, disposed of the whole of the Mulvaney gang, except the leader Mark Mulvaney, after they had massacred seven of his trail hands during a rustling operation on the Western Cattle Trail in Nebraska.

Mulvaney himself, a noted desperado, wanted for robbery and multiple brutal murders, is still at large. But his days are surely numbered. Mr Calhoun has dedicated himself, with the help of the law, to bringing the miscreant to justice. He told this paper that he believes Mulvaney is now leading a new gang which is operating in the Denver area. He said that Mulvaney is a coward at heart, who deserted his men to save his own skin, and the new members of his gang would do well to take note of this.

He also said that he feared that Mulvaney would flee when he heard that the man who broke up his gang was in the area. But wherever the outlaw scuttled away to hide, Mr Calhoun promised that justice would catch up with him in the end.

We wish Mr Calhoun the best of good fortune. This great country of ours must rid itself of unscrupulous villains like Mulvaney, who think they are above the law.

This paper understands that Mr Calhoun will be taking the stage to Pueblo on ... to investigate a report that the Mulvaney gang has been seen in that area.

'That's great,' said Blair. 'How soon can you get it in the paper?'

'In the edition that comes out the day after tomorrow,' replied Carling, 'but I'll need to know by tomorrow morning the actual date when you'll be taking the stage to Pueblo.'

'I'm going to see the station manager now,' said Blair. 'I'll let you know that date when I've seen him. Can I make a copy of this draft?'

'Sure,' said Carling, handing him a pencil and a sheet of paper. When Blair had made the copy, he walked along to the stagecoach station and introduced himself to Manley, the manager.

He showed Manley the draft of the news item and explained that about a week after it appeared in the *News* in two days' time, he wanted to take the scheduled stagecoach run from Denver to Pueblo. Confirming what the sheriff had already told Manley, he said that there would be two lawmen from Pueblo in the coach with him, both disguised as drummers, the commercial travellers of the day, and the sheriff would supply an experienced driver. The question was, for which day could this be arranged?

Manley studied some sheets on his desk before he replied.

'I've sold no tickets yet for the run ten days from now,' he said, 'so we'll make that the day and I'll make sure you three are the only passengers on the coach. As for the driver the sheriff mentioned to me, he's a good man. There ain't no problem over him taking the coach to Pueblo.'

'Good,' said Blair. 'I'll tell Carling I'll be on the stage leaving ten days from now. That's a Monday, isn't it?'

'A Monday it is,' replied Manley. 'You're fairly sure, then, that Mulvaney'll try to kill you?'

'Fairly sure,' said Blair. 'I've spent a bit of time in his company. I have a good idea of how his mind works.'

The news item duly appeared in a prominent position on the front page of the *News* two days later, and on the same day Manley confirmed the arrangements regarding the use of the stagecoach.

# THIRTEEN

The evening before Blair was due to join the Pueblo coach, the two deputies from Pueblo, both disguised as drummers, and carrying bags ostensibly containing samples of their wares, arrived by coach and Blair met them secretly in their hotel room. He complimented them on their disguises, then discussed the details of the operation with them. He warned them not to give any indication, before the coach left, that they knew him.

The next morning, the sheriff, and three deputies, assembled quietly on the outskirts of town, two hours before the coach was due to leave. They headed for a point in the foothills from which, using field glasses, they could observe the stage leaving Denver.

Back in town, two hours later, Blair and

the two supposed drummers boarded the stage. As it moved off, Blair saw a man, unknown to him, mount his horse and ride fast out of town, ahead of the coach, in a southerly direction.

Up in the foothills, Sheriff Riley saw the coach leaving and also the fast-moving rider in front of it.

'*There's* a man in a hurry,' he said. 'One of Mulvaney's men for sure. When he tells Mulvaney that there ain't a shotgun rider and the only other passengers on the coach are two drummers, I figure Mulvaney's bound to go for Calhoun.

'We'll shadow that rider,' he went on, 'instead of the coach. Then we'll know where Mulvaney's waiting.'

They rode parallel to the path of the rider below, keeping him under observation through field glasses. Two miles past the first way-station he slowed down and disappeared into a small copse of trees about four hundred yards from the road along which the coach would soon be passing. Riley rightly assumed that the gang was waiting inside the copse to attack the coach as it passed by.

The posse moved as far down the slope as they could without being observed. Then they waited for the coach, delayed by a brief stop at the way-station, to arrive. Riley, looking north through the field glasses, was the first to see it. He told his men to mount, and ride when he gave the order.

Inside the coach Blair and the two deputies, guns in hand, waited in readiness for an attack. As they came abreast of the copse, Blair saw four riders burst out of it, riding fast towards the coach. He shouted to the driver, who quickly brought the coach to a standstill, pulled the brake hard on, then climbed down from the box and joined the others inside. At the same time, Riley gave the order for the posse to ride down to the coach.

As the outlaws neared their objective they drew their hand-guns and started firing, two of them heading for one side of the coach, two for the other. The hail of accurate fire they received in return killed two of them instantly and badly injured a third. Mulvaney unhurt, turned to flee, but ran into the posse bearing down on him at full speed and was shot down as he tried to escape.

Riley ran to the coach door and opened it. 'Everybody all right in there?' he asked.

'Reckon so,' replied Blair, as he climbed out, followed by the others. He walked over to Mulvaney and looked down at him. The outlaw, cursing him, died as Blair watched.

They slung the three dead bodies over the backs of three horses and sat the wounded outlaw in the coach. Then they all returned to Denver.

Ned Carling excelled himself with a highly dramatic account of the operation and the paper's part in it, in the next edition of the *News*.

Mary Mariner was sitting at a favourite spot of hers, on the river-bank not far from the house. Of late, she had spent a short time here each day, weather permitting, dreaming of a future with Blair, and trying to fight off a growing feeling of apprehension that Mulvaney would triumph, and that she would never see Blair again.

Hearing a slight sound behind her, she jumped up and turned round. Blair, smiling, was standing in front of her. She felt an overwhelming sense of relief.

'It's all over, Mary,' he said, 'and everything's fine. Mulvaney's finished and I've collected a reward from Sheriff Blaney over in Fairborn that's going to come in mighty useful for us to get started on whatever we decide we want to do. I've come back to start on that courting business we talked about.'

She smiled at him. 'I've been waiting here a long time already,' she said. 'I figure there ain't no need for us to go through all that. How about you?'

'I feel the same way, Mary,' he said, 'but I

wanted to do things right. Can we start looking around for a preacher?'

'The sooner, the better,' Mary replied.

He kissed her. Then, hand-in-hand, they walked towards the house.